LOVE THY ENEMY

RED STONE SECURITY SERIES

Katie Reus

Cover art: Jaycee of Sweet 'N Spicy Designs
Editor: Julia Ganis, JuliaEdits.com
Author website: http://www.katiereus.com

Love Thy Enemy/Katie Reus. -- 1st ed.

ISBN-10: 1942447507
ISBN-13: 9781942447504

eISBN: 9781942447498

For my wonderful sister.

PROLOGUE

Six years ago

"Mom!" Dominique called out as she shut the front door of the crappy two-bedroom duplex they lived in behind her. She hated this place, hated that they'd had to move here after her dad's gambling debts had taken everything from them. Thanks to nonexistent insulation, she was pretty sure their new neighbors were dealing drugs too.

Everything was surprisingly quiet now, but it was noon. She figured the jerks next door were probably sleeping off a bender.

Her mom hadn't been answering any of Dominique's texts, though. And that wasn't like her. Not to mention her mom had missed work yesterday, according to the owner of the restaurant she waited tables at. When he hadn't been able to get a hold of her mom, he'd called Dominique, worried. The older man had taken both of them under his wing and had been trying to find them a better place to live.

Since she'd just graduated high school yesterday Dominique had celebrated by staying over at her best friend's house last night instead of coming home. The thought of coming back here had been too depressing and her mom had been okay with it. She'd said she was headed to work and that Dominique should have fun. For the first time in a long time she'd actually seemed happy.

They'd even talked about moving out of this place soon. Dominique had been saving from her part-time afterschool job and her mom had picked up extra shifts at work so they finally had enough to find somewhere safer.

"Mom!" she called again as she reached the living room. An empty bottle of cheap red wine was on the coffee table along with an empty bottle of pills. Xanax.

Panic punched through her as she raced down the hallway to her mom's room. Her mom had struggled with depression over the last six months. Understandably.

But Dominique had thought things were different now. Her mom had seemed so freaking happy yesterday... She stopped in her tracks outside her mom's open bathroom door.

The water in the tub was...dark. Red. Her mom's head was laid back against the wall, her eyes closed, her face unnaturally gray and one arm draped over the side of the tub. Dried crimson streaks trickled down the outside of the tub and stained the square black and white tiles.

Bile rose in her throat as terror streaked through her. She tried to force her legs to move, but couldn't cross the threshold into the bathroom.

"Mom?" The word just slipped out even though she knew her mom couldn't hear her.

She wasn't stupid. She knew her mom was dead. She wasn't breathing and that blood was from slit wrists. Stepping back, Dominique lost it, all the contents of her breakfast coming back up and onto the floor until she was on her hands and knees, sobbing and dry heaving.

When she eventually found the energy she crawled away from the doorway opening and collapsed back against the wall. With trembling fingers she managed to dial her older cousin Quinn. He'd been a cop and now worked for some big deal security company. She wanted him to help, not some random strangers, and she knew he'd call the police.

Her mom had cut that side of the family out of their lives because she'd been ashamed of how 'far we've fallen,' as she'd put it. It was stupid and Dominique didn't care about any of that right now. She needed help. She needed family.

She needed her mom not to be dead.

When Quinn answered the phone she lost it and started sobbing again.

She'd thought her dad dying was the worst thing that could have happened, but this was way worse. Her mom had *chosen* to take her own life, leaving Dominique all alone in the world.

CHAPTER ONE

Viktor Ivanov could barely hear what his acquaintance was saying as he stared at the tall blonde beauty he'd seen talking to various employees of Red Stone Security. She had a body made for pleasure and right now all he could envision was burying his face between her thighs, listening to the sounds she made as he made her come over and over.

He'd never had such a visceral reaction to anyone before—and he'd been with his share of beautiful women. Lately not so much, as even sex had started to become more of the same. That was what happened, he supposed, since he only employed escorts for sex anyway.

He managed to get in a few grunts of acknowledgement until Abram, his business partner/half-brother, subtly stepped on his foot.

Blinking, he turned back to Shane Hollis—the man who'd been bothering him the last ten minutes with inane conversation about an investment opportunity. The truth was, he didn't give a shit what this guy said. He wasn't going to do business with Hollis. He'd already bought some of the man's restaurants a year ago because Hollis couldn't manage his money. The trust-fund baby liked drugs too much, something Hollis didn't think Viktor knew.

Tonight Viktor had simply been trying to be civil because that's what normal people did. They behaved in certain ways because it was socially acceptable.

He hated it the majority of the time but he was a businessman. It didn't matter that he couldn't stand most people. He could put on an act. Most of the time anyway.

Tonight he couldn't stop staring at the curvy woman with legs that seemed to go on for miles. He wondered if she worked for Red Stone. Or maybe she was just friendly with the wives of the brothers who ran the company because he'd seen her talking to Elizabeth Martinez Caldwell a lot. Lizzy, as her friends called her, came from a very wealthy, influential family and she'd married one of the Caldwell brothers a couple years ago. They'd just had a kid not long ago too, something he remembered seeing in his files—because he kept files on anyone in the city who was important.

"She is not for you," Abram murmured next to him.

He blinked and realized he'd been staring again and that he and Abram were alone once more. Hollis must have left, thank fuck. If Viktor hadn't just invested in a new restaurant—that had a big display here tonight—he wouldn't even be here at the Celebration of Chefs. "Who?"

"Don't pretend. You and half the men here tonight are watching her. She works for Red Stone, I hear. She's not for you." Abram shook his head. "That kind of woman…she wouldn't look twice at men like us."

Viktor just grunted, dismissing his brother's words. The owners of Red Stone were fucking Boy Scouts and the people they hired were the same. That didn't mean he couldn't *speak* to the woman. Talking was harmless.

Mesmerized, he drank in the sweet lines of her body as she waved at a friend and said goodbye to the people she was talking to. When he saw her headed to speak to a couple he knew—the man, anyway—he straightened.

In her heels she was over six feet tall, a virtual goddess. Most women with that much height would choose to wear shorter heels, but she clearly owned who she was. He could see it in every confident step she took. Those curves were enough to make a man want to lock a woman down for a marathon of sex. And a woman who looked like that—he didn't think any sane man would want to let her go.

If she truly worked for Red Stone, it was...annoying. Maybe she was a former spook like the founder and one of his sons. She was young though, under thirty. Maybe even closer to twenty-five. It was difficult to tell.

When Rhys Maxwell, one of the people she'd been talking to, broke away from her and another woman, Viktor headed in Rhys's direction. He stopped next to the British businessman at a display of champagne glasses.

"Maxwell," he murmured, nodding politely.

The other man smiled, nodded. "Ivanov. Surprised you're here. Thought you hated stuff like this."

"Just bought a restaurant."

"Ah, that makes sense." Maxwell's gaze turned back to the two women, his interest in the shorter brunette clear. Unfortunately for Maxwell, Viktor was fairly certain the woman didn't plan on sleeping with him. He was good at reading people and her body language screamed she wasn't interested.

"Is that the same woman you brought to the last event?"

Maxwell turned to look at him, his expression turning slightly possessive. "Yes."

"Who is her friend?" The words came out harsher than he'd intended, but he wanted to know.

Maxwell blinked, seemed to relax at the question. "Ah, one of Raegan's friends. They work together." He tilted his head in their direction. "I'll introduce you."

A burst of anticipation hummed through him as they headed over, but as they started walking, the blonde darted away and into the crowd, moving with clear purpose. He was surprised by the disappointment that slid through his veins.

As they reached the brunette, he said, "Who is your friend?" The question came out demanding and he had to remind himself about those stupid social niceties, to act normal.

Maxwell cleared his throat, looked slightly annoyed at him. "Ah, Viktor, this is Raegan. She works for Red Stone Security. I believe you have some acquaintances in common."

He turned to look fully at the woman. She had an innocent quality to her and he could see he frightened her. Or at least made her nervous. He did that a lot to people without meaning to. It was his size. He was six foot five and big all over. He hid most of his tattoos, but some still peeked out and he couldn't do anything about the ones on the backs of his hands. Not that he gave a shit what people thought of him. Hell, most of the time he used his size and appearance to his advantage, especially in business. But he didn't want to frighten random women.

"It's nice to meet you." He smiled politely, held out a hand and was careful to shake her smaller hand gently.

"It's nice to meet you too." There was a wariness in her gaze as she eyed him before she dropped his hand and turned to her date. "Will you give me a few minutes?" she murmured to Maxwell.

Viktor's business acquaintance gave her a soft smile. "Of course."

Once she'd disappeared into the crowd as well, he turned back to Maxwell. "She doesn't seem like your type." Much too innocent and soft. And if the rumors were true, Maxwell had a darker side to him, liked rougher sex.

"She's just a friend," Maxwell said through gritted teeth.

Ah, so she was definitely not sleeping with him.

"She's Keith Caldwell's niece," Maxwell added.

Well that was interesting. He made a note to find out more about her. Anyone related to the Caldwells would be important enough to keep on his radar. Especially since Harrison Caldwell owed Viktor a favor. One he'd been sitting on for many years. Frowning, he wondered if she was the woman Porter Caldwell had contacted him about—the one who'd been drugged at one of Viktor's clubs. He dismissed the thought for now. He'd see when he reviewed the video footage.

"Who is the blonde she was talking to?" There was no point in pretending he didn't want to know. Not when he was certain Maxwell had figured out the only reason he'd approached the Brit was for an introduction. Even if they had mutual acquaintances, they weren't friends and didn't move in the same social circles.

"Name's Dominique. Works for Red Stone, but I'm not sure what she does." He lifted a shoulder, clearly not interested in the woman.

Which soothed something jagged and unexpected inside Viktor. His half-brother was right—she wasn't for him. He slept with paid escorts for a reason. It kept things simple, uncomplicated. The women he used went through an agency run only by women, and all the escorts worked there willingly and were paid well. It was illegal, sure, but he'd done a lot of illegal things in his life. As the son of a dead mobster, he'd learned young that the world operated in shades of gray. He couldn't remember the last time he'd used the escort agency, though. Over a year ago, at least.

A loud shout drew his attention to one of the restaurant displays. There were twelve celebrity chefs on site and anyone who was anyone in Miami was here. For the most part. The event was mostly outdoors in a park-type area. Twinkly lights and a huge gauzy canopy were high above everyone, strung between two buildings: an art center and a convention center.

He turned to see Grant Caldwell race toward the convention center, shoving a waiter out of his way as he ran. His two brothers, father and one of his brothers' wives were all behind him, moving at a rapid speed.

Maxwell murmured something next to him before hurrying in that direction. Viktor was mildly curious about what was going on, but the majority of his focus was on finding the woman again.

"We need to go," Abram said quietly, appearing at Viktor's side out of nowhere. Like a ghost.

Because that was what Abram did. He moved with an impressive stealth. Which was good for getting into places he didn't belong. "Why?" he asked, scanning the area, still looking for the blonde. *Dominique.* He wanted to say her name out loud, to feel it on his tongue.

He wanted to feel *her* against his tongue.

Annoyed with himself, he rolled his shoulders once.

"You have a meeting and I don't like whatever that just was." His brother frowned in the direction the Caldwell brothers had gone.

"Let's go. The display tonight..." He trailed off, feeling a little guilt that he hadn't paid much attention to their newest investment. The restaurant he'd just taken over had an exhibit here tonight—the whole reason he'd even come. And he'd been by only once to speak to the chef.

Abram nodded. "Good. Everything is good. Lucy has everything under control."

Viktor held back a snort. Lucia—who insisted they call her Lucy—was the new assistant they'd recently hired and he knew his brother had it bad for her. He looked at his watch. "Stay until the end of the event. One of us needs to be here and I want to make sure Lucy has an escort to her vehicle." The last part was true.

He could tell his brother wanted to argue, probably because he didn't want to be around Lucy even though he was attracted to her, but Abram would watch out for her because he cared for her and because they looked out for their employees. In the past more so than now, Viktor and Abram had engaged in…more than one illegal activity. They'd made enemies, so all of their employees could be potential targets. Especially one who worked so closely with them. They never forgot that.

Abram straightened stiffly. "I'll make sure she gets home safely."

Viktor nodded once and headed out. Going into business with Abram two years ago had been one of the best decisions he'd ever made. He hadn't even *known* he had a half-brother until three years ago.

He texted his driver as he headed toward the art center and away from whatever commotion had just happened. It was fairly late for a meeting, but there was a piece of property he'd had his eye on and the real estate agent couldn't show it until tonight.

The art center was silent as he stepped inside, his shoes almost completely noiseless as he headed down a long hallway that would exit onto a quiet side street. Instead of parking in the main garage attached to the convention center he'd had his driver drop him off. It made things easier when he wanted to leave. No traffic to deal with.

There were a few staff from the Celebration of Chefs and probably from the art center itself along the hallway, acting as 'security' so people wouldn't wander into closed display areas they weren't allowed in. But everyone was silent as he passed, simply smiling politely and nodding.

When he pushed open one of the glass double doors at the end of the long hallway, the salt-tinged, slightly humid Miami night air rolled over him. The heat of summer could be sweltering during the day but at night it was more than bearable, especially with the breezes.

Not that he cared about any of that when he spotted the tall, sexy Dominique talking quietly to a man around her height. At least with her heels they were the same height. They were standing near a built-in bench along the sidewalk next to a cluster of palm trees. Even though it was evening there were enough lights around the center, including one nestled in the palm trees, to illuminate her perfectly.

When she shifted her feet he realized there was another woman next to the man. A petite brunette with Mediterranean coloring who was tucked up against him, her arm wrapped around his waist. They were all murmuring quietly.

The goddess had her back to him, showing off the sweet curve of her ass and her toned calves. It was like she'd walked out of his fantasies. Her long, blonde hair cascaded down her back in big waves and he wondered what it would be like to run his fingers through them. To wrap his fingers around a thick section and hold her head back, nibble along her neck and jaw before he claimed her mouth.

What the fuck is wrong with me?

Beautiful women in Miami were a dime a dozen, but she was...stunning. There was no other word for her. Something about her poise and confidence called to him. The way she walked and moved was like...a goddess. Like she didn't give a fuck what anyone thought about her.

As if she sensed him watching, she turned around. Her dark eyes widened, then just as quickly narrowed in clear anger.

At *him*.

He stilled, watching her carefully. Her reaction to him was unexpected. They'd never met. That much he was sure of. He didn't date. And she was someone he'd never be able to forget.

Her jaw clenched as she watched him for a long moment, the anger there so clear, so potent, he felt it like a body blow.

She broke eye contact first, turning away from him, her body language changing in an instant. Her back was ramrod straight and he could practically feel the tension rolling off her.

Frowning, he headed in the other direction to where he knew his driver was waiting, but he kept her in his peripheral vision.

Only once he was inside the back of the armored vehicle did he text his half-brother. *Find out who the blonde is. Her name is Dominique. I want everything you can dig up.*

He wanted to do the checking himself but Abram was a genius with computers and getting into places he didn't belong. While Viktor could eventually find out what he wanted, Abram would do it in a quarter of the time.

Right now he wasn't feeling patient where she was concerned. He wanted to know what the hell he could have done to warrant such a reaction from a stranger.

Consider it done.

His brother's responding text soothed a fraction of the tension surging through him. But he wouldn't be satisfied until he found out exactly who she was. And until he met her in person.

CHAPTER TWO

"You don't have to stay and help. I'm fine getting out of here by myself."

Abram watched as Lucy slid the clean champagne glasses into the storage container. She was so methodical in everything she did, so damn organized. She was the best thing that had ever happened to him and his brother. Business-wise.

Because if his brother had ever looked at her in a sexual manner, Abram would have lost his mind. Which was stupid, because she was just an employee.

He placed a hand over hers, even though he knew he shouldn't. Touching her was dangerous to him. To her as well. He had no business wanting her, for too many reasons. The least of which was that she worked for him and his brother. But mainly because she was too good for him. He'd told Viktor that the blonde from earlier wasn't for him and he hadn't been kidding. He knew he should take his own damn advice, but... "And you don't *need* to even be here anymore. The restaurant staff should be cleaning up." He ground out the last couple words, beyond annoyed that she was still here. She worked too hard as it was.

He glared at one of the waitstaff of the fusion restaurant he and his brother had just acquired. They were getting paid double overtime for this event tonight. He'd had to take a phone call and when he'd come back he'd found Lucy helping with the breakdown of the tables, moving around like the Energizer bunny.

"Hey, I tried to tell her she shouldn't be helping. *Three* times." The employee whose name eluded Abram held up his hands in mock defense before he went back to stacking the tea light candles. "Maybe she'll listen to you," he tacked on.

Abram nearly snorted. Doubtful. She never seemed to stop, no matter what task she took on. She was a dark-haired little pixie. Her espresso-colored hair fell in a sharp bob around her face. Usually she kept it stick straight but tonight there were soft waves in it and she had some sort of sparkly headband on. It should have looked ridiculous but it just made her look like a fucking princess.

Another reminder he had no business wanting her. She was too sweet and innocent for him.

She pulled her hand away from his, frowned up at him. Even in her four-inch heels she was only five feet four inches. "The faster we get this done, the faster everyone gets out of here."

"It's not your responsibility. They're getting paid handsomely for tonight. Now let's go. Viktor made me promise to get you home safely." Using his brother as an excuse usually worked.

Her expression softened then. "That man is so sweet. Fine. Let me grab my bag."

Abram gritted his teeth as she turned away, the fluffy skirt of her blue strapless dress twirling out as she moved. There were little sparkles in the skirt too. His brother wasn't sweet, but Lucy seemed to think he was a big teddy bear. It was ridiculous. With him? She usually just seemed frustrated. He didn't understand why.

She pulled a big black bag she called a purse out from behind one of the folded-up tables. It was her 'work bag' and he'd rarely seen her without it. The thing was so big he was surprised she didn't topple over with it. On instinct, he plucked it from her hands.

She let it go with a sigh and he was glad she didn't argue. By now she probably knew it was pointless.

He grunted, hoisting it onto his shoulder. "What do you have in this thing?"

"I can carry it for you if it's too heavy," she murmured, giving him a mischievous look.

God, what he wouldn't give for a taste of her. Just one. "I think I can manage."

"If you say so."

He found himself grinning at her slightly sarcastic tone. At least she didn't seem annoyed with him anymore. The woman made him crazy. "Did you get enough to eat tonight?" He knew she usually skipped lunch and basically seemed to exist on caffeine.

She snorted. "I didn't get anything. I meant to, but got too busy. Hey, why are we going this way? My car's in the parking garage."

"I had one of the guys take it back to the office for you." It was a company vehicle so they all had keys to it. "Viktor wanted to make sure you got home safely tonight. My driver will take you."

"Oh...thanks." There was an odd note in her voice, one he couldn't define.

"Besides, I heard you say you wanted to see the Sanchez exhibit. I asked one of the staff from the art center if we could check out the display and they're allowing us in before we leave," he said as he opened the door to the art center. But he would make sure she got something to eat on the way home.

Sanchez was an up-and-coming photorealist artist in Miami. Abram didn't give a shit about art but he could appreciate the man's talent. The images were all of places in Miami or Florida and had soul.

Lucy blinked up at him, paused in the open doorway. "That's very nice." Did she have to sound so surprised by that?

He lifted a shoulder, uncomfortable with the way she was watching him.

She gave him a soft half-smile he felt all the way to his core. "Thank you."

It took a moment for his legs to catch up to his brain. He fell in step with her in two strides then had to slow down because of their height difference.

After walking through the exhibit—which she seemed to thoroughly enjoy—they finally left the art center. His current driver, Kir, was waiting by the curb, just like he'd instructed.

He held open the door for Lucy before Kir could get out and do it. When he slid into the backseat after her, she looked almost surprised. Maybe she hadn't realized he was coming with her. He didn't care that Viktor had just said to make sure she got to her car safely. He was making sure she got *home* safely. There wasn't even a threat against them at the moment, but he still wanted to take care of her. *Because she is a good employee*, he told himself. That was it.

"Does he know my address?" she murmured, strapping herself in.

He nodded, strapping in as well before telling Kir to head out.

"Did you have fun tonight?" she asked, her dark gaze on him.

"It was fine." The bright city lights played over her delicate features as they drove toward downtown.

Her mouth quirked up. "That's not really an answer."

"It was...business. Not for fun." Fun would be stripping her naked, making her come, seeing her lose control. He didn't do relationships. He'd never had time, but lately he found himself thinking he'd make an exception for Lucy. Which, again, was stupid since she was an employee.

Now she shrugged. "So? You can still have fun at events."

He'd seen her talking to a multitude of people tonight, some clearly for business, but others he knew she was friends with. Because everyone seemed to adore Lucy. It was hard not to. "It was fine," he said, repeating his earlier statement. He felt stupid and tongue-tied around her. Always.

She gave him one of those frustrated looks and started to respond when her phone dinged from her giant bag, indicating an incoming text. Instantly she reached for it.

"You don't have to worry about work anymore. It's okay to go off the clock." He worried that she might burn out. Maybe they were working her too hard?

She laughed as she responded to the text. "When you and Viktor slow down, I'll slow down."

He swallowed hard, looked out the window. It was doubtful he and Viktor would slow their pace anytime soon. Money gave him security and some days he couldn't seem to make enough. Abram had grown up poor, unlike Viktor. But it didn't matter. Viktor'd had it bad too. Abram was glad he'd only had limited contact with their father when he was young. After he'd turned eight he'd cut off all contact with the bastard, told his mom he didn't want to see him again. Thankfully his mom had been more than happy to, even though it had meant cutting off any support from the sperm donor.

He'd assumed Viktor was just like that monster but he'd found out differently when he'd started to dig into him more. Only then had he approached him and had been surprised Viktor had no clue about his existence. It had taken time, but they'd eventually become friends.

Best friends. The first one he'd ever had. Abram didn't trust many people. Just some of the guys he'd served with from his Marine Corps days. And his brother. No one else.

When he realized Lucy was still texting, he plucked the phone from her hands.

Letting out a soft gasp, she stared at him. "What are you doing?"

"You're done for the night."

"Damn it, Mr. Ivanov—"

"Abram. My name is Abram," he gritted out. She called his brother by his first name. But she'd never called him by his first name. She either completely avoided using his name, or when she was annoyed called him Mr. Ivanov. It was ridiculous and made him insane.

She let out a frustrated growl. "I know that. Please give me my phone. I just need to respond to one thing and then I'm done for the night. Promise."

"Say my name and you get your phone."

She blinked at him, her cheeks flushing pink. "What?"

"My first name. Say it." He knew he was pushing her, should probably stop. But he didn't care. He felt practically possessed right now with the need to hear her say his damn name. He was also aware of Kir watching him in the rearview mirror curiously.

"Fine, Abram. Can I have my phone now?" She held out her palm, her hand slightly trembling.

He frowned, wondering if he'd frightened her, but...he didn't think so. Her eyes were slightly dilated and her cheeks were still flushed. She almost looked aroused, but that couldn't be possible. The woman couldn't seem to stand him some days. He gave her the phone. "Don't call me Mr. Ivanov anymore. If you do I'll start calling you Lucia."

She simply gave him a dark look as she took the phone and didn't respond one way or another. For some reason she didn't like her given name, but he thought it was beautiful. It fit her.

As she continued to text, he looked out the window at the passing lights and traffic. He should have just walked her to her damn car. Not given her a ride home. Being around her always put him on edge, made him feel awkward. Maybe he should limit his contact with her even more. Normally he just emailed or texted her with instructions about work but sometimes working with her directly was unavoidable.

The truth was, though, he looked forward to the time they did spend together. Even if she seemed perpetually annoyed with him. Or aloof, which was even worse.

* * *

When he saw the number on screen he answered the phone after three rings, forcing himself to remain patient. "Yes?"

"Abram has definitely taken an interest in the new assistant. He followed her around all night." The man snorted in amusement.

"Are you in a secure place?"

"Of course. I'm at a park. No chance of anyone overhearing."

"Good... What else do you have?" Because that wasn't enough. He'd seen that himself over the last couple months. And Abram wasn't the one he hated. It was Viktor, with his smugness, the way he looked down on him. The man thought he was better than him. Which was ridiculous. Viktor's father had been a common criminal, a thug.

"That's it for now. You wanted me to call with updates on them." His contact sounded annoyed.

"What about Viktor?" He couldn't keep the disgust out of his voice.

"What about him? He never brings women around."

He knew that. Viktor seemed to prefer paying whores, which was no use to him. He needed to find the man's weakness and a woman would be the best one there was. Men became stupid over women. He didn't let his disappointment show. "This is good. Thank you for the update." Even though it wasn't what he wanted, he liked to keep his contact happy because he never knew when he might get something useful.

"I'll be in touch when I have anything else."

He ended the call. There was no need to talk any longer. He'd approached the man he'd been using for information because he knew of the man's secret addiction to strip clubs. Pathetic, really. Spending all that money for nothing except some grinding and maybe a blow job in a back room.

But the man was risking a lot by crossing the Ivanov brothers. They'd been careful though. No one would ever figure out he was getting information on them, building up a reserve of information he might be able to use.

Because Viktor would pay for taking from him.

CHAPTER THREE

Dominique glanced up as her boss, Porter, stepped out of his office. He'd been here earlier than her this morning, which was pretty unusual, especially for a Monday.

Their two offices were connected by a big door and they both had huge windows overlooking the city. The elevators opened right up into her office space where she was the basic 'guard' for Porter. Not that he really needed one. He oversaw one of their security divisions so the only people who ever came to see him were employees directly under his purview. Or potential new clients, but he usually met with them in one of the conference rooms down the hall.

"You don't have any meetings until ten," she reminded him. It didn't matter that she updated his online calendar—and had synced it to his email account and phone so he got hourly alerts—he still sometimes forgot stuff. He'd once told her it was because he was getting old, which was ridiculous since she was pretty sure he was only thirty-four. She had a feeling his forgetfulness had more to do with his one-year-old son who hadn't been sleeping through the night lately.

"I know. I forgot to tell you I've got someone coming in. It has to do with what happened to Raegan. Would you get some coffee and refreshments for us?"

"Of course," she said, automatically standing. "Do you have news about who drugged her?" Her friend had been drugged on Friday night. And Raegan was Porter's cousin so of course he'd be involved in finding out what happened to her.

Too much had happened over the weekend. Raegan had been drugged—and almost taken by some random guy at a club—but thankfully someone had been there for her. A 'sexy cop,' as Raegan liked to call him. Dominique had no idea what was going on with those two but she had a feeling she'd find out all the details soon enough. She was just glad Raegan was okay.

"No, but I'm hoping to get something this morning," Porter answered.

"Any news about what happened Saturday?" Raegan had been almost attacked at the Celebration of Chefs, as well. Dominique had missed most of the commotion because she'd been out front talking to her cousin.

He shook his head, his expression grim.

"Do you think...the two things are related? Raegan didn't say, but I thought maybe, I don't know. It seems like a coincidence that two bad things like that happened to her so close together."

"I...don't know. We're looking at the events as if they might be connected. The cops are doing what they can, but we've got better resources. The guy who's meeting me has a video of Friday night. I want to go over it. You were there too so if you wouldn't mind looking at it, I'd appreciate it."

"Of course. Anything I can do to help. I'll go grab those refreshments and be back in a few minutes. What time—

" She stopped talking as the elevator doors whooshed open and Viktor Ivanov stepped out.

Seeing him made a sharp burst of anger pop inside her, but she shoved it back down. She was a professional and she'd worked very hard to get a job like this. She wasn't going to ruin that because she couldn't control her temper. Even if she did want to punch Ivanov right in his perfect, chiseled face. This must be the meeting Porter had been talking about.

Of course. Ivanov was the owner of the club Raegan had been drugged at. It made sense he would be here. But he looked more like a thug than anything else. The no doubt custom-made suit he had on didn't hide the fact that he might as well be a street brawler. His dark hair was more or less a buzz cut, cropped close to his head, and his blue eyes were icy. She could see a few tattoos peeking out under the cuffs of his jacket and the ones on his knuckles were always visible. She'd heard the rumors that he'd once been part of his father's criminal organization in Miami. When his father had died he'd supposedly gone legit, but she didn't buy it.

She pasted on her best smile and hoped it didn't look too fake. "I'll grab the coffee," she murmured to Porter as she nodded politely at Ivanov—who was staring intently at her—and left her office. Her heels clicked against the tile as she headed down the hallway to the community kitchen they shared with the other offices on this floor. Red Stone owned the entire building and they didn't rent out offices to anyone else so everyone here was a vetted Red Stone Security employee.

When she stepped into the kitchen she was glad it was empty. Right now she didn't feel like exerting any energy to make polite small talk. After starting a fresh pot of coffee, she pulled out the tray of muffins, cookies and scones they kept on hand for impromptu meetings. Everything was fresh, replaced daily. Once she had the refreshments set up on the rolling tray she headed back to her office and tried to ignore the nausea churning in her stomach.

Seeing Viktor Ivanov just reminded her of everything his family had taken from hers. From what she'd heard, he was just as bad as his dead, gangster father. She couldn't believe Porter was meeting with the man, but to get video of the club where his cousin had been attacked…yeah, she would meet with the devil too if it would help her friend.

When she rolled the cart into Porter's office, she found both men sitting in front of Porter's laptop. Porter paused the video as she entered and both men stood.

It annoyed her that Ivanov was being polite and standing for her—and still watching her with those intense blue eyes. She ignored him and smiled at her boss. "If you want I can set up the projector in the conference room for the video. You'll be able to see everything more clearly."

He nodded once, his expression still tight. "That'd be great, thanks."

Leaving the refreshment tray, she exited the office, able to breathe again now that she was out of Ivanov's presence. She usually towered over most people, or was at least the same height as most men in her heels, but not him. She hated that.

It was rare that someone made her feel off her game, but he did. After what his family had done to hers, what his father had done to her mother... She swallowed hard, shoved all those thoughts aside as she focused on her job. She could get through this morning then he'd be gone and she'd never have to see him again.

Unfortunately, an hour later she found that not to be true. Porter and Ivanov walked back into her office as she was getting off a phone call.

"Dominique, if you can spare the time, would you mind walking Mr. Ivanov out? He has some questions about Red Stone and I told him you're the best person to answer anything." He smiled, a genuine one as he turned back to the big thug. "I don't know what I'd do without her."

Ivanov half-smiled. "I have an assistant like that as well. She keeps me in line." There was just a hint of an accent in his voice.

She knew he'd been born in the States, was an American, but his father and she was pretty sure his mother had both been born in Russia. It explained his slight accent.

Even though she wanted to say no, there was no way she ever would. No matter her feelings for this man, she would do her job. Porter had placed a lot of faith in her the last few months and she'd already gotten one raise. She wasn't going to screw this job up. Smiling, she stood from her desk.

"Of course. Don't forget, ten o'clock."

Porter blinked once, letting her know he actually had forgotten, then nodded. "Right. I've got everything ready to go."

He'd been part of the security team for so long that she guessed transferring to a more admin position had been an adjustment for the former Marine.

Keeping her fake smile in place she nodded at Ivanov and motioned toward the elevators. "So what would you like to know about Red Stone?" *Ugh.* She hoped he wasn't looking to hire the company. Though she wasn't sure they'd even take him on. Porter's dad, the founder, had an intense vetting process, even for their clients. He didn't take on known criminals, no matter how much money they had.

"How long have you worked for them?"

She cleared her throat as she stepped through the open elevator doors. "About five months."

"You were with Porter's cousin on Friday night." It wasn't a question and no doubt he'd seen her on the video.

She cringed at the thought of her boss seeing her out dancing on that video. She hadn't been drunk or doing anything stupid, but still, it felt a little weird. If she'd known that Ivanov had owned the club she'd gone to with her friends, she'd have never gone. At least he'd been willing to give Porter the video feed in an effort to find out who'd tried to take Raegan.

"Yes." The elevator started moving moments after the doors closed. She stood next to him, trying to ignore his presence. It was hard, considering what a giant the male was. He was crowding into her space without even trying. His cologne was light and she hated that he smelled good. If he was anyone else she might have even…checked him out. Which just annoyed her even more.

"I'm sorry your friend was drugged. I've already fired the security staff from that night."

Surprised ricocheted through her at his words and for the first time since getting in the elevator she looked over at him. "Seriously?"

He frowned, his gaze flickering to her mouth. "Why are you surprised?"

She lifted a shoulder, not liking what she saw in his icy blue eyes. She'd been on the receiving end of lust from males since she was fourteen. She could tell he liked what he saw when he looked at her and it pissed her off. When the elevator doors opened on the bottom floor she pushed out a sigh of relief, belatedly realizing her reaction was a little too obvious as they stepped out of it. "Did you have any questions about Red Stone?" Because she didn't want to talk about herself or Friday night.

"Have we met before?" he asked. She could practically hear the frown in his voice, but didn't meet his gaze as they crossed the main lobby.

Smiling, she nodded at two of the security men behind the huge circular reception area. She knew they were both armed to the teeth. "No."

"Then what have I done to offend you?" he demanded softly.

Surprised by the bluntness of his question, she looked at him. He'd stopped walking so she did the same. "Why would you say that?" She wrapped her arms around herself.

His expression was hard, the angles of his face sharp and defined. He looked every inch the ruthless business-man everyone said he was. "Because of the way you looked at me Saturday night."

Damn it. She was hoping he hadn't remembered or even noticed her. She'd been unable to rein in her reaction to him though. She took a steadying breath. "If you do business with my boss it won't be a problem. I'm a professional." She didn't want to be on Viktor Ivanov's radar in any way, shape or form, but...

Staring into icy blue eyes so similar to his father's, she was close to losing it. When she looked at Viktor, she saw blood and death, her lifeless mother in her tub. And it made her want to cry.

"Your family disgusts me," she gritted out before turning on her heel. She couldn't be around him any longer, couldn't fake being polite. Though clearly she hadn't done a good job of that anyway.

* * *

Viktor scrubbed a hand over his face as he read over the file his brother had given to him. It was very thorough. He couldn't get rid of the image of Dominique's almost scared expression when she'd looked at him. He was used to people being afraid of him.

But he'd hated that she'd looked at him like that. Which was stupid, since he didn't even know her. Maybe it was because, more than fear, he'd seen raw pain in her gaze.

Now he knew why.

He closed his eyes. "Fuck," he muttered.

"You had nothing to do with it." Abram's voice was whiplash sharp. As always when he was annoyed.

"My family—our family—owes her a debt." He looked up, sat back in his desk chair.

Abram was half sitting on the front of his desk, his arms crossed over his chest. "Bullshit. Her father had gambling debts. No one held a gun to his head and made him go to Ilya for that loan."

Even now Abram wouldn't say 'my father' or 'our father.' It was always Ilya. "When her father died the debt should have been settled with the life insurance and the house." He looked down at the files again, saw how much the life insurance and house—which was on the beach and was prime real estate—had been worth. It hadn't been quite enough to cover the debt because Dominique's father had racked up an obscene amount. "I think Ilya took the rest of the debt from Dominique's mother. Probably through sex."

Abram shifted uncomfortably on the desk before shoving to his feet. "We can't know that."

No, but Viktor could read between the lines. His father, gangster that he'd been, had kept impeccable records. "Even after her father died the debt was paid down in credits." He tapped a finger against the old file even though Abram already knew what it said. He was the one who'd discovered that Dominique's father had been in deep to their own father. "Not money. You know what that means. Then her mother kills herself six months later?" It was clear why. His father had been a monster, had probably driven Dominique's mother to suicide with his sick demands she'd been forced to fulfill.

"I wish he was alive so I could kill him," Abram muttered, clearly referring to Ilya. He went to the big window that overlooked downtown, and was silent as he stared out of it.

Viktor didn't respond, just flipped over the current page and stared at Dominique's mother. She had Mediterranean coloring as well as dark hair, and according to the file she'd been five feet five inches. It was clear Dominique favored her father in height and hair color, but she'd gotten some of her mother's traits as well, including a beautiful face.

He felt almost sick to his stomach. Dominique had lost her father and mother in less than a year and could trace both deaths back to his father. No wonder she'd looked at him as if she wanted to claw his eyes out.

He pressed the intercom on his phone. "Lucy, can I see you for a sec?"

Moments later his new assistant strode in, not a strand of her short, dark hair out of place. As always her gaze strayed to Abram for a fraction longer than necessary, but his brother had his back to her and didn't turn at her entrance.

"There's a property that's part of our rental program," he said, scribbling down the address. "I want it taken off immediately and all current reservations cancelled. We'll refund everyone and have Rita try to relocate them to another rental property of ours. If she can't, still comp them wherever they end up staying and include something extra for the inconvenience. A bottle of champagne, whatever. I want this done by the end of the day. No excuses from Rita."

Normally Lucy did whatever he said without question. Now her eyes widened a fraction. "Rita's going to lose it," Lucy said, a small grin tugging at her lips.

"She can deal with it." Rita was the real estate agent for Abram and him, and in charge of almost all of their company's properties. "But because you'll have to deal with her bitching, take her out to dinner one night this month. Anywhere she wants. No limits."

Lucy's grin widened. "I have a feeling you might regret that when she orders a two-thousand-dollar bottle of champagne."

He just snorted because Lucy wasn't kidding. "Probably so. Just make it happen." He didn't care how much it cost him to fix this.

"I will." Still grinning, she left, pulling the door shut behind her.

Abram turned around then, his expression unreadable. "Are you doing what I think you're doing?"

"We owe her."

His lips flattened, but to Viktor's surprise, Abram didn't argue. "What you're doing is insane."

He lifted a shoulder. He'd done a lot of shitty things in his life, but seeing the face of one of his father's victims—maybe she hadn't been victimized directly, but Dominique's life had been impacted greatly because of Ilya—made him need to act. To pay her back somehow. Nothing could bring back her family but he was still going to try to make things right. "You think I'm wrong?"

"No. I just don't think she's going to take what you're offering."

Maybe not, but he would still try.

CHAPTER FOUR

"What's going on with you?" Porter's voice made Dominique jump in her chair and nearly knock her bottle of water off her desk.

She steadied it with one hand, her heart beating faster than normal. "Nothing. Why?"

He eyed her curiously. "You've been acting off since that file was delivered. What's in it?"

Damn it. Of course he'd get straight to the point. After seeing Viktor Ivanov yesterday she'd been feeling out of sorts and then the file she'd received this morning had completely knocked her world off its axis. She didn't know what to think of it—didn't know why Ivanov had sent it to her. "It's personal."

Porter gave her a pointed look. "I know that. What's in it?"

"I'm...not telling you." She felt bad, but she just couldn't.

He frowned and sat on the edge of her desk. "If you need help with anything, you just have to ask." The true concern in his voice nearly undid her.

But she couldn't tell him what was in the file without telling him more about her past. Okay, considering how hard she'd been vetted, she figured Porter already knew about her past, but still, that didn't mean she wanted to talk about it. Even if she did open up to him, she couldn't do that without crying. No way in hell was she going to break down here and in front of her boss. Talk about mortifying and unprofessional. Red Stone Security was a male-dominated workplace, and while she loved her job she didn't want to be seen as anything other than professional. And crying at work? Not happening.

"I'm good, promise... Has my work been suffering today?" She'd been on autopilot all morning and now felt really guilty. If she'd been slacking she'd make up for it tomorrow.

He blinked. "What...no. Jeez, Dominique. I'm talking to you as a friend, not your boss. You're on top of everything as usual. I just want to make sure you're okay. With what happened to Raegan I think we're all a little on edge. I just wanted to make sure things are good."

"I swear I'm fine. I...would you mind if I left work an hour early today? I skipped lunch, so—"

"Just go now. I'm about to clear out anyway. We can afford to sneak out early one day."

The truth was, this week was one of their slower ones. All his guys were on long-term security jobs for the next month so her duties were standard and she could do them in her sleep. That would change in a few weeks when the guys started moving to new contracts. Still, it felt weird to leave early, but she was going to do it. For her sanity, she needed to. "I really appreciate it."

Once he'd returned to his office she shut down her computer and headed out. Instead of leaving, she rode the elevator up a few floors to Lizzy's floor. To her surprise, Lizzy's assistant got her in to see Lizzy almost immediately.

"Hey, chica. What are you doing up here?" Lizzy was stretched out on a chaise lounge with her laptop next to a window instead of sitting at her desk. And she was wearing yoga pants and a T-shirt.

"Is there a new dress code I don't know about?" Dominique laughed as she headed over to the chaise and perched on the end of it.

"Ha ha." Lizzy was sitting cross-legged and slid her laptop to the side. "I can't go to the gym after work so I ran up and down the stairs during my lunch break. Just haven't had time to change and since I don't have meetings today I'm staying comfy."

Dominique figured that Lizzy could pretty much do whatever she wanted, and not just because she was married to Porter. The woman was one of their online security experts and a more than decent hacker. In fact, Dominique had heard some of the guys call her scary good. Something she was really hoping for right now. "That's a little insane."

Lizzy shrugged. "If I don't let the energy out, *I* go insane."

"Fair enough... Can I ask you a favor that you can't tell your husband about?"

Lizzy's expression turned serious. "Depends on the favor."

"It's not work related. I just...need to know where someone is right now. I need to talk to him and it has to be in person."

Lizzy frowned, absently pushing back a loose strand of her long, dark hair. "Why not call this person?"

She could. Heck, she probably should. But no, this needed to be an in-person conversation. Dominique needed to see Ivanov's face, gauge his reaction. "It's...personal." Dominique was friends with Lizzy but she never forgot that Lizzy was also her boss's wife. Shaking her head, she stood. "I know I'm putting you in a weird position and that I'm asking you to invade someone's privacy. Can we just forget I asked—"

"Who do you want to track down?"

She shifted from foot to foot, debating if she should just leave, but she really wanted to know where he was. And to talk to him right freaking now. "Viktor Ivanov."

Lizzy blinked in surprise. "Is this about Raegan?"

"Not remotely. Nothing to do with her, the club, or work. It's very personal. This is his number." She held out a sticky note she'd scribbled the number on earlier.

Lizzy gave her a mischievous grin. "Personal, huh?" She pulled her computer back into her lap and her fingers started flying over the keyboard at an alarming pace.

Dominique wanted to correct her, to tell her not personal in the way she implied, but held her tongue as Lizzy worked. When she started to move around to see what her friend was doing, Lizzy shook her head.

"Uh-uh. Just sit down while I work. Plausible deniability, my friend. If you don't see what I'm doing, you can't admit to any wrongdoing." She didn't glance up once as she said it, her expression almost gleeful.

"Are you breaking the law?" It was a dumb question. Of course Lizzy was. Dominique had heard the rumors, knew that Lizzy could pretty much hack anything. It was the whole reason she'd come to see her.

Lizzy just snorted then grinned. "He's at one of his hotels." She rattled off the name and address, but Dominique
already knew where it was.

She'd lived in Miami her whole life and knew the city
well. "Thank you."

Lizzy didn't look up, just typed in a few more com-
mands. "Looks as if he's currently in the ground-floor restaurant. East side. Well, his personal cell phone is. I'm
assuming it's with him."

Dominique blinked. "You're terrifying."

"Thanks," Lizzy said, looking up. "Are you in trouble?"

"No." She felt like a mess though. "It's just personal. I
promise."

Lizzy slid her computer to the side and stood. "What I
know about Ivanov isn't much, but I've heard enough that
he's a dangerous man."

She nodded. "I know."

"Be careful."

"Thanks. I will. If, uh, he leaves, will you call me? I'm
headed over there right now."

"I'll keep an eye on his phone and let you know. Do
you need an escort or anything?"

She shook her head. She didn't need an audience for
this, didn't want anyone to know her personal business.
None of her friends from work knew what had happened
to her parents—or if they did they'd never brought it up—
and she planned to keep it that way. She didn't want pit-
ying looks. "If you need to tell Porter about this, it's okay."

Lizzy just nodded, which wasn't really an answer
whether she was going to tell her husband or not.
Dominique didn't really care though. She needed to talk

to Viktor Ivanov right now and ask him why the hell he'd sent her a contract signing over the rights to her childhood home. He supposedly just wanted to give it to her.

For free.

There had to be a catch. Even if there wasn't, she sure as hell wasn't taking it. She was going to get to the bottom of this and find out what the heck he was up to. Because a man like Ivanov wouldn't give away such a valuable piece of property for nothing.

* * *

Dominique was a mix of nerves and anger by the time she made it to Viktor's hotel. Or one of them, apparently. She'd known he was successful, but when Lizzy had said 'one of his hotels' she'd realized that he must be wealthier than she'd thought.

She had her car valeted because she couldn't even think about dealing with parking. After a confirming text from Lizzy that Ivanov was still in his restaurant, she headed into the lobby. The decorating was minimalist but everything was high-end. A huge chandelier hung right in the middle of the foyer of the five-star boutique hotel, glittering prettily above everything. She was almost certain the place didn't have more than a hundred rooms. The interior had an Old World feel to it and was truly beautiful. She'd read about it in one of the luxury publications she kept up to date on for Porter. She just hadn't realized Ivanov was the owner.

Before she'd taken two steps, a man wearing black pants, a white button-down shirt and a simple black jacket with the hotel's logo on it approached her, a warm smile on his face. "Welcome. How may I help you?"

She gave him one of her most winning smiles. She hadn't really thought this through before coming down here. She'd just been so impatient to see him and hadn't wanted to wait—or call. For some reason that had seemed intimidating. Now, she realized, seeing him in person after she'd told him that his family disgusted her was nerve-racking. Gah, what had she been thinking? "I'm here to see Mr. Ivanov."

Before the man could respond another man appeared as if out of nowhere, moving silently across the marble tile as he approached. She'd seen him at the Celebration of Chefs on Saturday with Ivanov and thought they might be business partners. He was just as big and definitely as intimidating as Ivanov. The man smiled at her, sort of, and dismissed the hotel employee with a few short words.

"I take it you're here to see my brother, Miss Castle."

She blinked at his words, surprised he even knew who she was. "You're Viktor's brother?" She hadn't realized that he had any siblings. Once upon a time she'd done her research on him too. But that had been years ago, when she'd been obsessed with finding out everything about the man who'd destroyed her family. She'd moved on since then, had avoided reading anything about Ivanov once his father died.

"Half-brother. He's working but he'll make time for you." Without waiting for her to respond he turned on his heel and headed toward the open entrance to a restaurant. There was a sign outside that said it was closed until four o'clock.

"I can come back later," she said as she hurried to catch up with him. Looking at the man now it seemed obvious he and Viktor were related. He was just as big, with similar blue eyes. He even had a similar haircut, buzzed close to his head. "I should have called."

He stopped as they reached the entrance. "How did you know he was here?"

Feeling her cheeks flush, she just shrugged. "Lucky guess."

He gave her an assessing look before turning away again and motioning for her to follow him.

She gritted her teeth at his rudeness, but whatever. She'd just shown up here without calling—after illegally tracking Ivanov down. Dominique wasn't going to throw stones about manners.

He led her across a mostly empty restaurant with white tablecloths on all the tables except a circular booth Viktor was sitting at. There were two men about ten feet away from him, standing quietly by the bar. His bodyguards, she guessed, if the way they sized her up was any indication.

His half-brother held up a hand to them, said something in Russian she didn't understand. Unlike Viktor, he didn't have an accent when he spoke English.

Viktor stood, his eyebrows raised as he looked at her, his gaze sweeping her from head to toe. There was a mix of lust thrown in too, which completely screwed with her head.

He started to say something, then one of the men said something under his breath to the other one in Russian, the look the guard gave her easy to define. She might not understand the language but the way he leered at her made her skin crawl.

On instinct she took a step back but to her surprise Viktor moved into the guy's personal space, getting right up in his face. It was amazing—he didn't even touch the guy but it was clear he didn't have to. The guard's body language showed fear, if the way he tried to shrink back in an attempt to be invisible was any indication. Viktor murmured something too low for her to hear, but whatever it was, the man paled a deathly white and nodded once before practically running from the restaurant. He gave her a wide berth and avoided eye contact as he left.

The remaining man looked just as uneasy.

"Leave us," Viktor said to his brother—whose name she still didn't know—and the remaining man.

Once they were gone, he motioned that she could sit across the booth from where he'd been sitting.

She swallowed hard, wondering why she'd thought it was a good idea to just show up here. Viktor was huge and had a ruthless reputation. Clearly she needed to get her head on straight. She paused, unsure if she should sit or not.

"You don't have to be afraid of me," he snapped.

She jumped at the harsh tone.

He scrubbed a hand over his face. "I'm sorry. It's been a long day. Please sit."

Pushing out a breath, she did—because she wanted answers. "Why the heck did you send over that contract to me this morning?" The question came out as a half shout, making her cringe at herself. "Sorry, I'm just... Well, why did you?"

He was sitting ramrod straight, looking uncomfortable as he watched her. As if he didn't want her here any more than she wanted to be here. "It has come to my attention that my family owes you a debt."

She clenched her jaw tightly. A *debt*? A house wouldn't come close to making up for what she'd lost. "So you're just offering to give me my childhood home?" A place that held a lot of good memories. It was like he was dangling the best carrot ever in front of her but there was no way she could take it.

He nodded once.

"In exchange for what?"

He blinked. "Nothing. It's a gift."

"You can't offer a gift like that and think I'm going to believe you want nothing in return!"

He shifted against his seat, looking uncomfortable. Something told her he wasn't often uncomfortable. "I don't want anything. It's yours. I didn't get much from my father when he died, but your parents' house was part of my trust. I didn't...know what he'd done until yesterday."

Even if he sounded sincere she still didn't know if she believed him. And she regretted coming here. She should have just ignored the contract, ignored everything. Especially since it seemed clear that he must know about her parents, about her mother. It made her feel vulnerable in a way she hadn't in a long time. "I don't want it."

"It's yours. My father hurt a lot of people." There was a strained note in his voice, but she didn't know him well enough to be sure. "I know the house doesn't make up for *anything*, but I can't keep it. Not now. It's been on a rental

program for years since it's on the beach. It has high rat-
ings and does well in the summers so if you do the same
thing with it you'll make a nice yearly income from it. I
can recommend a property management company to run
it if you'd like."

No. This was not happening. The world didn't work
this way.

Unable to find her voice she abruptly stood. She didn't
want the house, didn't want anything from him and it
pissed her off that he thought giving her the property
would somehow make up for what his father had done.

And yet, part of her felt conflicted. He was supposed
to be a monster just like his father, and now she didn't
know what to think. She turned, ready to run out of
there, when his hand lightly clasped her wrist.

She turned back to him but wouldn't meet his gaze.
Instead she stared at his broad, muscled chest. Now she
was glad he was taller than her so she didn't have to look
into his eyes. And she hated that she noticed how attractive he was.

"Please take it," he murmured. "Sell it, do whatever
you want. But take it." There was a sort of desperation in
his voice, as if he meant every word.

He just wanted her to take it so his conscience could
be eased. And that wasn't going to happen. "That
house...is the last place I remember being happy with my
parents." Her voice broke on the last word and to her horror she started crying.

No! This was even worse than crying at work. Breaking down in front of the man she'd thought was a monster
for so long, a man who was supposedly giving her such a

huge gift with no expectations—she tried to rein in her tears, but when he made a distressed sound and awkwardly patted her on the back in a half-hug she couldn't stop herself no matter how hard she tried.

Almost against her will she found herself leaning into the very man she'd always thought of as her enemy.

CHAPTER FIVE

Viktor had never felt more at a loss in his life. He had no experience with crying women. He didn't know if she wanted any comfort and he didn't want to risk her shoving him away if he pulled her into his arms. Even if the thought of holding her close was something he'd been fantasizing about. No matter how stupid. So he awkwardly patted her back. If she was his he'd do more than this—he'd pull her into his arms, wipe away her tears and bring her pleasure, make her forget why she was in pain.

"Do you want to sit?" he murmured. Maybe he never should have sent that contract over. Maybe he should have contacted her first. But he hadn't thought she would want to see him or talk to him. Not after their last meeting. He'd just wanted to make things as right as he could. Upsetting her was the last thing he wanted to do, but clearly he'd made a mistake.

She nodded and swiped away her tears before collapsing on the edge of the booth seat.

Instead of sitting across from her he grabbed a chair from a nearby table and sat in front of her.

Her pretty brown eyes widened slightly but at least she wasn't crying anymore. There was still some dampness on her cheeks and he wanted to wipe it away, to touch her soft skin, take her pain away. But he didn't.

In his periphery he saw his brother reenter the restaurant. When he met Abram's gaze his brother tapped his watch. Viktor shook his head. He didn't care about his upcoming meeting. This was more important.

His brother's expression darkened but Viktor turned away from him and focused on Dominique. "The last thing I wanted to do was upset you," he said quietly.

"I think I believe you." She gave him a half-smile he felt all the way to his core. "I'm sorry I thought you were just like your father."

"It's a fair assumption." One most people made. For the most part people weren't wrong, at least not when it came to business. He *was* ruthless. He just wasn't a gangster and he didn't get off on hurting women. Unlike his father. "I'm sorry about your parents."

At his words her expression shuttered but he could see pain in her eyes. She couldn't hide that. And he wished his father was still alive so he could kill him all over again for what he'd done. "You know what he did to my mother?"

"I can guess." Because his father had been a monster. It was the reason he'd killed Ilya. Something no one knew. Not even his brother. He'd do it again too.

"I only found out after she killed herself." She swallowed hard and paused. He wanted to comfort her but didn't think she would want his touch. "She wrote me a letter. He...he said he made videos of them. So even after she'd paid off his bullshit debt he said she had to keep 'servicing' him or he'd put those videos on the internet for everyone to see." Tears tracked down her cheeks again and the sight was too much.

Fuck it. He couldn't sit here and do nothing. He pulled her into his arms and to his surprise she leaned into his hold, burying her face against his shoulder as she laid her hands gently on his chest.

He closed his eyes for a moment, savored the feel of her leaning against him, almost as if she trusted him. "I'm so sorry."

She sniffled and pulled back, wiped at her face. "It's not your fault. Even if I wanted to make you out to be a monster too." Guilt flickered across her features.

"I'm still sorry. If he was alive, I'd kill him." The words came out savage. Instantly he wished he could take them back when her eyes widened in shock. But screw it, he was who he was. There was no need to hide it, especially since he'd never have a chance with her. Not now. Not with the history between their families.

"I can't tell if you're joking," she said, giving him a watery half-laugh.

He wasn't, but wasn't going to tell her that. The only times he'd killed had been in self-defense, but not many people knew about that. They suspected, sure. Which was another reason for his reputation. "Please take the house."

She was already shaking her head before he'd finished. "I can't, but thank you anyway."

Viktor reined in his frustration. He couldn't very well order her to take it even if that was exactly what he wanted to do. He was going to make sure it ended up in her hands. After reading the file Abram had given him he'd learned that she lost her college savings fund because of her father's gambling, as well as her trust. She'd paid her way through college working two jobs and had only acquired minimal debt—which she'd just recently paid off. She had a strong work ethic, something he admired. Before he could respond he saw Lucy headed his way.

Viktor knew his brother had likely sent her in here because of the stupid meeting he needed to get to. He wanted to wave her away, but simply couldn't do that to Lucy—something Abram knew. She smiled politely at Dominique before focusing on him. "Abram wanted me to remind you that you've got that meeting to get to."

"Reschedule it. Reschedule everything this afternoon."

Lucy simply nodded and left.

Dominique's tears were completely dried as she looked at him. "I should go. I've taken up too much of your time. I really am sorry I judged you so harshly. It was incredibly unfair of me to lump you in with your father."

"It's fine." It wasn't like he was a good man.

"No. It's not." She took one of his hands, squeezed it once before standing.

Everything inside him stilled at the feel of her touching him. He wanted more and hated that he didn't have a chance with her. He stood with her, not wanting to let her go. "If you ever want to see the house, I'm not going to be doing anything with it. It'll be waiting for you whenever you're ready."

Her full lips pulled into a thin line as she sighed. "I'm not going to change my mind, but thank you. I'll show myself out."

Viktor just nodded and watched her leave, even if he wanted to escort her out simply to spend a few more minutes in her presence. But that was stupid. She might not think he was a monster anymore, but she would never look twice at him as a potential...*boyfriend* seemed like such a juvenile word. Regardless, she wouldn't look at him as a love interest.

He closed his laptop and headed out. His brother could deal with the rest of the day's meetings. Viktor was too edgy.

A run and a swim and maybe some time on the punching bag might expel some of this energy. But he doubted it.

He needed to get Dominique out of his system but he wasn't sure how. He hadn't even had a taste of her, yet thoughts of her consumed him. She hadn't seemed to think he was a monster after today so maybe...he did have a chance with her. Maybe they could be friends. He nearly snorted at the thought.

Even if he didn't have a shot with Dominique, he'd call later to check on her, to try to convince her to take the house again. Why didn't he believe his own lie? He wanted to see if she'd let him take her to dinner, to get to know her more. He'd give her a day then test the waters.

Walking away from her was something he just couldn't do.

* * *

"Here's the paperwork to fire Peter." Lucy set the stack of papers on Abram's desk, a half-smile tugging at her very kissable lips.

As if she was trying not to smile.

"What's that look?" Abram frowned as Lucy stepped back.

She blinked. "What do you mean?"

"You look...happy. Are you glad we're firing him?" Abram had been planning to anyway, but today's behavior had been the final straw.

Peter had been hired as professional security and had thought it okay to make a rude, sexual comment about a woman he didn't know, right in front of her. It didn't matter that Dominique couldn't speak Russian—Peter didn't know that. For all he knew she could have been a client. That kind of behavior wouldn't be tolerated.

"Why? Are you going to judge me if I say yes?" Now she was full-on grinning. "I don't even care," she said before he could answer. "I hated that guy. I'm so glad Viktor is firing him."

Abram frowned at her words, an alarm bell going off in his head. Lucy seemed to like everyone, even the most obnoxious of their clients. She was sweetness and fucking sunshine almost all the time, usually to people who didn't deserve her warmth. "You never said anything."

She shrugged, taking another step back toward the door. They'd been all over Miami today at various properties they owned, including a hotel he and Viktor favored. He figured Lucy would be leaving soon. Or he'd tell her to. It was well past time she called it a day.

"If I complained about every jerk who made me feel uncomfortable when he looked at me, I wouldn't be able to work anywhere. He was just one of those guys you know is a pig, so I'm glad he'll be gone." She lifted her phone at an incoming text, frowned at it as she typed in a response.

Feeling irrationally territorial, Abram stood from his desk. "He made you feel uncomfortable?"

"What...yes. And now he's gone. Or he will be." She gave him one of those megawatt smiles that were rarely reserved for him. "Hey, I'm gonna grab dinner at the diner down the street before heading back. Want to come with me?"

It was the first time she'd ever asked him and he'd be a fool to say no. Nodding, he grabbed his cell phone from his desk. "Sure. What do you mean, heading back?"

"I've got some stuff I want to get ahead of before tomorrow. You've got three meetings, and after today Viktor has way more on his plate because he cancelled his afternoon meetings." He could hear the slight question in Lucy's voice but would never talk about his brother's personal life to anyone.

"Are we working you too hard?" he asked as they headed for the elevators. This late in the evening the place was almost empty.

She frowned, smoothing a hand down her black pencil skirt. One that showcased her perfect, pert ass. Today she had on five-inch red heels that defined her calves. Calves he'd love to have resting on his shoulders while...

"No, why?"

"If we're not here, you shouldn't be here."

She snorted. "Abram, I love my job so stop worrying. You guys pay me great, and yeah I work crazy hours but it's worth it. Eventually we'll need to hire someone else but for now I'm good."

The sound of his name on her lips for the second time ever—the first she'd said it all on her own—made everything inside him go still as they stepped into the elevator. He finally found his voice as they reached the bottom floor. "If someone ever makes you feel uncomfortable at work again, let me know." There was no room for argument in his voice and he knew it sounded more like an order than a request but he didn't care. He'd wanted to say something back in his office about it, but then she'd asked him to join her for dinner and he'd pretty much lost the ability to talk. He knew she was just asking because he was the only one here, but still, a guy could dream this was more for her.

For a moment, his adorable pixie gave him a confused look. "Oh…ah, okay. I will, promise."

He nodded, taking her answer at face value, but he still planned to do another look at their newer hires. They'd made a mistake hiring Peter. On paper he'd been perfect, but at work he'd been subtly rude and not exactly lazy, but also not an outstanding employee. Abram and his brother owned a variety of companies and had enough different investment properties that they couldn't vet everyone. But the people who worked directly for them better be exemplary. They'd earned their reputation for a reason and they couldn't afford to look weak now. Not ever.

And if anyone ever made Lucy feel uncomfortable or even looked at her wrong? They were gone.

* * *

"Viktor appears to have a new weakness," his contact said quietly into the phone.

There was some sort of thumping in the background, a vibration. "Where are you?" he demanded.

"I'm in a bathroom at a strip club," he said after a moment. "The door's locked. No one is in here with me. You want what I got or not?"

"What's his new weakness?" He didn't want to get his hopes up, but a rush of adrenaline surged through him.

"Not a what, a who. A blonde woman. I'm not sure who she is yet. She met with him today at one of his hotels. Abram seemed to know her too. Viktor fired one of his security for saying something to her. I don't know the whole story, but Viktor also threatened him with dismemberment if he even looked at her again. That's what I heard anyway. After she left, he cancelled all his meetings and worked out for three fucking hours. It was like he was in a rage." There was a touch of fear in his voice.

This could be what he'd been waiting for. "You don't know her name?"

"No, but I snapped a picture of her when she left. She's fucking hot. Tall, blonde, killer body and full lips I could imagine sucking my dick."

He rolled his eyes. He didn't give a shit what the woman looked like, just how he could use her against Viktor. "Send the picture to me."

"I'll text it as soon as we hang up."

"This is good. Keep me updated if you see her around more. I'll wire you our normal fee." This information was definitely worth what he paid the man.

"Thanks." He could hear the glee in his contact's voice.

The man only cared that he got paid, which was good for him. As long as that loser kept feeding his stripper and God knew what else habit, he'd keep feeding him information.

He just hoped this woman truly was a weakness to Viktor—that he'd finally found something to use against the untouchable Ivanov.

CHAPTER SIX

Dominique picked up her cell phone, then set it down. Again. Next she picked up her glass of white wine and took a sip as she stared out over the balcony of her condo. The complex's pool was surprisingly quiet this evening.

She'd been on autopilot again today at work and for the first time ever had actually been counting down the clock until she could go home.

Her friends had their own stuff going on right now and even though she knew she could talk to them about anything, she didn't want to. She'd always kept her past private and while she figured her boss knew about her family, considering Red Stone's vetting process, she didn't like to broadcast that painful part of her life.

Now...she had a chance to own her childhood home, a place that held so many wonderful memories. It felt wrong to take Ivanov up on his offer because it was such a huge gift.

And after doing some research—some of which Lizzy had helped with—she'd found that yes, he was pretty ruthless when it came to business, but he didn't appear to have his hand in any illegal things. Lizzy said at least not anymore, but that he may have at one time. He also gave a lot to charity, specifically ones that supported education and literacy. Which shouldn't matter. But it did.

Even after meeting with him yesterday she'd wondered if her judgment was off, if he really was just like his father. But from everything Lizzy had found it seemed as if he'd hated the man. And he'd seemed so sincere when he'd been talking to her yesterday. She couldn't help but wonder if her judgment was off because of her growing attraction to Viktor.

She picked up her phone again and dialed his number. It rang once and she almost hung up but he answered immediately.

"Hello?"

"Mr., uh, Viktor. It's Dominique Castle."

"I know."

"Oh, right. I...just wondered if the offer to see the house was still open?" Because even if she didn't take it, she still wanted to see it. Maybe it would give her a sense of closure on that part of her life.

"Of course. Did you want to see it tonight? I can meet you there or pick you up."

His question and offer made her pause. She desperately wanted to see it, but... "I can drive there myself and I'll be telling a friend where I'm going and who I'm meeting with." After yesterday, some intrinsic part of her trusted him, but meeting with a man she didn't really know somewhere alone in the evening? Yeah, she was going to be smart about it.

Thankfully he didn't seem insulted at all as he let out a short, amused laugh. "Good. I'll be bringing my assistant as well. I'll be there in half an hour."

She couldn't believe how easy this was, how accommodating he was being. She'd expected to have to wait—

and she hadn't expected the small thrill at the idea of seeing him again. Which felt insane. "Thank you."

Once they disconnected she stared at her phone, wondering what the heck she was doing. Viktor Ivanov wasn't a man she should be attracted to, but she couldn't wait to see him face to face. And it had nothing to do with the house.

* * *

Viktor stepped out of his office, not surprised to see Lucy still at her desk. He knew she had plans to leave soon since it was well after seven, and he hated to ask her to work even later but he wanted her with him for this meeting.

"Lucy, would you mind coming with me to visit one of our properties? I'm meeting a woman there and think she'd feel more comfortable if you were with me."

"Is this the same blonde from yesterday?" Lucy asked, her smile just a little mischievous as she stood.

Over the last couple months Lucy's relationship with him had become a little more relaxed. He'd never had employees comfortable enough to treat him like anything other than a boss and he'd never had female friends. But he liked the dynamic of their relationship. "Maybe."

"I knew you liked her," she said, her smile growing wider as she pulled her purse out of one of her desk drawers. "I saw you checking her out at the Chef event. I'm never wrong about these things."

Lucy was far too observant—which was one of the reasons he'd never regretted hiring her. "It's not like that." Even if he wanted it to be. "We are...acquaintances."

She snorted as Abram stepped out of his office, a frown on his face. "Where are you two going?"

"To show Dominique the house."

Lucy's eyes widened slightly. "The one right on the beach you had Rita cancel all those rental reservations for? That place is gorgeous. Are you selling it to her?"

His brother was the only one who knew why he wanted to give it to Dominique, not sell. That wasn't something he'd share with Lucy or anyone else. "Something like that."

"I'll come with you," Abram said, stepping back into his office.

"No." Viktor didn't want his brother there. That would only make Dominique uncomfortable.

His brother stared hard at him, the tension between them clear.

Lucy cleared her throat. "I'll meet you downstairs," she murmured, her heels clicking as she hurried out into the hallway. Abram's gaze strayed after her for just a moment, the longing in his eyes clear. Viktor didn't think his brother would ever make a move on her, and not just because he was her boss. He seemed to view Lucy as unattainable. Viktor could relate to that sentiment.

"You don't want me with you?" Abram asked once they were alone.

"Not tonight."

"What if this woman wants to hurt you? You don't know that she doesn't blame you for our father's sins. Maybe this is a plot to lure you there alone."

Viktor sighed, scrubbing a hand over his face. He was glad his brother cared enough to be concerned, but he wasn't worried about Dominique trying to attack him. "You think I can't handle myself against a woman?"

"I think your judgment is clouded. This house is worth so much..." He trailed off, shaking his head. "I understand why you're doing it, but what if the offer insulted her and now she wants to hurt you?"

"Is this about me bringing Lucy?" Because his brother couldn't seriously think he'd be ambushed by an untrained woman.

Abram just clenched his jaw.

"Well?" Viktor demanded.

"I think we're pushing her too hard. She's putting in seventy-hour workweeks with us. And now you're bringing her with you when she should have left an hour ago? I want to hire another assistant so she doesn't burn out."

Ah, so it was about Lucy. "I agree. You want to tell her or should I?"

Abram lifted a shoulder. "Maybe you should. And she should be the one to approve the final hiring—after we've vetted them."

"Agreed." Lucy would be working closely with whoever they hired so they would need to get along. His brother was right too. They had been pushing her too hard. Some days he felt as if all he did was work. But he'd rather be at the office than go home to an empty house or out to some bullshit event where he didn't like most of the people there to begin with.

As expected he found Lucy waiting downstairs in the lobby, talking with one of the security guards. And as usual she was a chatterbox on the way to the beach house, talking about what they had on the books for the rest of the week and the next, some figurative fires he and his brother specifically needed to put out and other stuff he half listened to.

He was glad she was talking, filling the space with noise so he could try to ignore the anticipation humming through him at the thought of meeting with Dominique.

It was completely stupid to be excited to see her, but after she'd been so visibly vulnerable yesterday she'd gotten even further under his skin.

When he steered into the driveway he saw she was already there, leaning against her car. She had on sandals, white shorts that showed off miles of her tanned legs, and a flowy summer top. It was clear she'd come straight from home or somewhere not work. The last two times he'd seen her she'd been wearing professional dresses that came to just below her knees. Though nothing could hide her incredible body.

He nearly groaned at the sight of her, but kept himself in check. "Once we're inside, can you give us some privacy?" he asked Lucy quietly even though Dominique couldn't hear him. Yes, he'd brought Lucy to put Dominique more at ease but he could admit that he wanted time alone with her. Didn't matter if he didn't have a shot with her. A deeply buried part of him wanted her to see him as a man and not a threat.

"Of course."

Dominique had pushed away from her car and was standing at the front of his SUV, her body language nervous. When he got out, she forced a smile, clearly uncomfortable.

"Thank you for doing this." He hated that uncertain note in her voice.

And he wanted her to just take the damn house. He didn't understand why she was being stubborn about it. She'd only said she wanted to see it tonight. She hadn't mentioned anything about taking ownership.

"It's no problem," he murmured, trying not to stare at her. "Dominique, this is Lucy, my assistant."

After they made polite introductions, he asked Lucy to open the front door and told her they'd be inside in a minute.

"She just thinks you're a potential buyer," Viktor said. "I didn't tell her anything about who you are or why you're here." Though he knew Lucy was curious because there was no sane reason to sell this place. Not when it was making the company a lot of money.

Dominique let out a short sigh and gave him a small, appreciative smile. "Thank you." She turned to look at the huge, two-story house and he allowed himself to drink in her profile.

She'd pulled her long hair up into a tail and she wasn't wearing much makeup. She looked different than she had Saturday night and in her work clothes. A little younger than he'd originally thought—though he knew she was twenty-five now from his files. And a lot more vulnerable. When she wrapped her arms around herself and shivered he knew it wasn't from the July weather. He wondered if being here hurt her and he hated that it was a possibility. He didn't know how to comfort her though. Or even if he should try.

"If it's too hard to go inside we can come back later. Or I can just give you a key and you can come by whenever you want." It would probably be easier on her that way, going inside alone.

Her head snapped around to look at him. For a long moment she watched him with a wealth of emotions bleeding into her dark gaze, one of which was anger.

Which surprised him. His brother's words came back to haunt him and for the briefest moment he wondered if she did want to hurt him in some way. Not that he was worried about her physically taking him on.

"Part of me hates how nice you're being," she finally whispered. "I hated you for a long time. I thought...you were just like him." She turned away before he could respond and headed up the walkway to the front door.

Scrubbing the back of his neck he followed after her and tried not to watch the sway of her perfect ass. Tried and failed.

What the hell had he been thinking, coming here? He should have just let Rita or Lucy handle it. Or just sent the fucking key straight to Dominique.

Being around her and knowing she likely only tolerated him was torture. Especially when all he wanted to do was kiss her.

* * *

Dominique sat on the edge of the queen-sized bed in her old room that looked nothing like it used to. A leopard print comforter with giant throw pillows covered the bed. An oversized canvas print of palm trees and the ocean hung on the wall above the dresser and small television. As far as beach rentals went, it was nice. The decorator certainly liked loud prints and colors, if the other rooms were anything to go by, but she could see the appeal for renters. For them it was a fun place to stay in for a week or two.

It had been a wonderful place to grow up in. Closing her eyes, she had a flash of her mom standing in the doorway, telling her that she'd made double chocolate chip cookies and that Dominique better grab some before her father ate them all. Her mom had loved baking. She'd tried new recipes practically every week. Their house had always smelled like cookies.

That was before everything had gone wrong.

As stupid tears pricked her eyes, she angrily swiped them away. She'd been here too long tonight. She knew she should just leave but hours later, she couldn't seem to force herself out of this room.

Part of her was irrationally angry at Viktor for offering her this, for dredging up a bunch of old memories she'd done well to keep locked down. But she knew that was stupid. He didn't seem to have any hidden agenda, just a need to make things right. If anything, he seemed almost desperate for her to take the house, something she still wasn't sure about.

At a slight noise in the doorway she nearly jumped when she saw Viktor standing there, looking almost hesitant. Now that she didn't hate the man she could truly appreciate how attractive he was. She might have compared him to a thug before, but the truth was she *liked* that look.

He had a darker edge to him that she found insanely sexy. His dark hair was cropped close to his head and those eyes—she could definitely get lost in that pale blue gaze. His height and build were enough to make her weak in the knees. Not many men towered over her and she liked that he did. Her experience with sex might be lacking but she had a feeling he'd know what he was doing in the bedroom. How could he not? The man was always in total control and built like a—

He cleared his throat and she realized she was staring at his mouth. Great—she was totally perving on him at the most inopportune time.

"I had one of my drivers pick Lucy up. It's getting late and she's got early morning meetings."

Which meant he probably did too. Of course. Cringing, she stood. "I'm sorry. I didn't mean to take up—"

He shook his head sharply. "Don't be sorry. I just didn't want you to be surprised when you realized she was gone. I can wait outside for you. Take as much time as you need."

"You're very thoughtful." She hated that the words came out as an accusation. But around him she felt like a mess. It was hard to reconcile him with the man she'd always thought he was.

To her surprise his lips quirked up, softening his expression just a bit. "You're the first person to ever say that to me."

She couldn't feign surprise at that. He seemed like a hard man, and in business she knew his reputation was brutal. "This used to be my room," she said, changing the subject. "Though I had posters of surfers on my walls." She half-smiled, looking around the transformed space. "And my walls were purple."

"You surf?" He took a few steps into the room.

"Not really. I mean, I did in high school a little. Longboard, mostly. The posters were of surfer guys. *That* was where my interest was back then."

He snorted, the sound taking her off guard. "That wasn't so long ago."

She lifted a shoulder. "Eight or nine years. God, it feels like a lifetime ago... I hated both of them for a long time," she blurted.

He stepped farther into the room and, to her surprise, sat on the bed next to her. "Your parents?"

"Yeah. My dad for getting killed in a stupid bar fight and leaving us. Then my mom for... I was such a spoiled teenager. Well, not too terrible, I guess, but I was pretty self-involved. I loved my mom but I only cared about getting out of that place we were living in, about spending time with my friends. I hated what happened to us, hated that I got stuck in a new school for my last year of high school because we couldn't afford my private school anymore. I never really thought about how much it affected her. I used to think if I'd paid more attention I'd have known that something was really wrong, that she..."

Dominique swallowed hard, lifting a shoulder. She couldn't finish the sentence. It was hard enough thinking it, let alone saying it out loud.

"She was your mother. She was protecting you. It's what mothers do." He reached out and swiped his thumb across her cheek.

Dominique hadn't even realized more tears had slipped past her defenses. The feel of him gently touching her almost undid her completely, but he quickly dropped his hand.

"You sound like you know that from experience."

He looked straight ahead instead of at her. "My mother died when I was seven. My memories of her are...good ones. She was a sweet woman who got involved with a very bad man."

The pain in his voice was so raw she squeezed his forearm on instinct, wanting to comfort him somehow. When he stiffened under her touch she pulled back, not wanting to make him uncomfortable. And she felt a little bad at noticing how incredibly muscular he was and wondering if the rest of his body was just as toned and ripped. She was pretty sure he was, because it wasn't like his suit hid how strong he was.

Looking away from him, she said, "When I was five I wanted a princess party, complete with a prince and princess." She wasn't sure exactly why she was telling him other than she wanted him to know what this house meant to her, what his offer essentially meant. "The 'prince' got food poisoning or something at the last minute so my dad stepped in and wore the costume and stayed in character the whole time. The party was by the pool here, including a pink princess house, and all my friends got princess costumes and tiaras to wear and take home. It was so ridiculously over-the-top for a five-year-old." She shook her head, laughing slightly. "My dad was always like that with everything. He grew up poor so I guess he just...I don't know." She sighed, swiping at more tears. "I swear I'm not normally a crier."

Viktor wrapped an arm around her shoulders, his hold almost awkward, but she appreciated it. Hell, she needed the comfort right now. She leaned into him, trying to ignore that spicy masculine scent that went straight to her head. He was just becoming more and more attractive to her every moment.

"You can cry all you need." His accent was slightly thicker now.

She laid her head on his hard shoulder, soaking up some of his strength. "You really are nothing like I expected," she murmured.

"I don't hear that a lot." His voice was dry. "Usually people say I'm worse than they expected."

Laughing again she lifted her head to look at him. Their faces were only inches apart, making her suck in a breath at the close proximity of his mouth.

His very kissable mouth.

She swallowed hard, stared into those intense blue eyes. For a long moment she wondered what it would be like to kiss him, to feel his lips on hers. That thought would have seemed insane a day ago. Now...

He cleared his throat and whatever weirdness was going on between them was instantly broken.

"My father was nothing like yours," he said quietly, looking straight ahead again, his posture stiff.

Something about the way he was almost awkward was...sexy. Something she shouldn't be thinking about. "Even with...you? Was he not a good father?"

He let out a harsh laugh, the sound full of bitterness. "When I was fifteen he threw me into a ring with one of his fighters to 'toughen me up,' as he put it—he ran an illegal fighting ring for about a decade. The guy went as easy as he could on me without making it too obvious. He didn't want to kill me, but I ended up with a broken nose, three broken ribs and..." He trailed off, shaking his head. "At least you have good memories with your family."

She was too shocked to respond. How awful to have such a brutal man for a father.

"Take the house, Dominique. It's the best 'fuck you' to my father you can make. Take it and do what you want with it."

Forget the house. She wanted to reach out and comfort him somehow.

As if he sensed her thoughts he abruptly stood and headed for the door.

"Have dinner with me tomorrow night?" she blurted. When he turned to look at her with raised eyebrows she continued. "To talk about the contract." Which, okay, was a complete lie. She wanted to spend more time with him. That knowledge disturbed her but she couldn't fight the pull toward him. The house was something she didn't even want to think about right now.

He nodded, his eyes flaring with heat, and she wondered if he felt that same pull. She knew he wanted her, had seen moments of awareness from him, but it could be nothing more than just lust. "I can meet you somewhere."

"Or you can just pick me up. I'm guessing you know where I live by now?" It should annoy her, but he was trying to fix what his father had done. Considering that he'd sent her that contract, it wasn't hard to figure out that when he'd done research on her, he would have found out more about her. Her address and phone number were probably at the top of the list.

His face flushed, the action...almost adorable. The man really was ridiculously sexy. "I'd have to look it up, but it's in the file I had put together on you."

"I feel like I should be mad about that."

His mouth curved up ever so slightly. "You should be. Though...you found me at my hotel so you've done some research too." There was a hint of a question at the end. As if he'd been wondering how she'd done that.

Her face heated at his words. She wasn't going to admit that she'd asked a friend to locate him.

"Is seven o'clock good?" he continued when she didn't respond.

"It is." The tingle of excitement in her belly was ridiculous, she told herself. But that didn't matter. She was already thinking about what she'd wear tomorrow night.

Because she wanted to get to know sexy and dangerous Viktor way more than she should.

CHAPTER SEVEN

Abram wasn't sure what he'd done to piss Lucy off, but in the last hour she'd been giving him the cold shoulder—and he had no idea why. Last night he'd been annoyed with his brother for taking Lucy with him and she'd no doubt sensed the tension between him and Viktor. But things had been normal between Lucy and him today. They'd even had lunch together. Sure, Viktor had been with them, but things had seemed like they always did.

And now he felt like a fucking fifteen-year-old girl, obsessing over her. He scrubbed a hand over his face as she stepped into his office, her expression perfectly neutral. It annoyed the hell out of him.

"I'm about to head out. Do you need anything else, Mr. Ivanov?"

He gritted his teeth at the formal title. There was no doubt she was pissed at him now. "What did I say about using my first name?'

She rolled her eyes. "I'll take that as a no. Have a good night."

He was out of his chair and around his desk before she'd taken one step back to the doorway. "What's going on with you? What did I do to piss you off?" Because he was racking his brain and he couldn't think of anything that made any kind of sense.

"Nothing, sir. I'm just—"

"Cut the shit, Lucy."

Anger flared in her dark eyes but she seemed to rein it in. "I'm sorry if I have an inappropriate attitude. I'll make sure to—"

"No, you're not sorry. What the fuck is going on?" he demanded, practically shouting. He was close to kissing her senseless. Anything to get a reaction out of her.

She didn't flinch at his show of temper, something he adored about her. Just put her hands on her hips and glared up at him. "Am I going to get fired for being honest with you?"

"No. And when are you *not* honest?" One of the reasons why she was such a good fit for Viktor and him was that while she was almost always in a good mood, she also didn't put up with their shit. And she wasn't afraid of them. They'd had assistants in the past who jumped anytime they gave an order. It was ridiculous.

"You are such a dick sometimes! I get why you act that way in business, because you and Viktor have built something amazing. But I overheard your conversation with Viktor an hour ago." She was fuming and he didn't understand why.

"So?" He hadn't shut the door to Viktor's office when he'd gone in there. The conversation hadn't been confidential. Viktor was going out with Dominique tonight and Abram was worried about him getting hurt. That woman might have an ulterior motive, for all he knew. It didn't matter that Viktor was his older brother—Abram wouldn't let anyone hurt him. Viktor had gone through enough over the years.

"Oh my God, I want to smack you. 'Do not go out with her, Viktor,' 'She is not the type of woman for you,' 'She just wants to hurt you.'" She repeated some of the things he'd said to his brother, her impression of him mocking.

He blinked. "Is that supposed to be me?"

"It's what you sound like. Why don't you want your brother to be happy? I've heard you say the same kinds of things to him before!" She stomped a heel, as if she was going to advance on him. Which he found insanely hot. "What kind of woman do you think is right for him? Because I did a little research and before you get on your high horse, just *don't*. I know you have files on tons of people," she continued before he could respond, and there was nothing to say anyway because it was true. "I *knew* she looked familiar so I made a call to a friend at Red Stone."

He blinked again. "You did?"

"Of course I did. You're my guys. I look out for both of you." Before he could fully digest what she'd said, she continued, her rage against him clearly building. "She's a freaking exemplary employee over there and a model citizen. They wouldn't have hired her if she wasn't. So what's wrong with her? And why do you always tell your brother that a certain type of woman isn't right for him? Do you mean women who *aren't* escorts? Because that's pretty shitty, Abram! He deserves more than an escort."

His gaze narrowed. "You know about that?"

She rolled her eyes again, throwing her hands up in exasperation. "Of course I know. I did my own research on both of you before I even applied here for a job. I'm not an idiot." She poked him in the chest with a fingertip.

"And I like him. He's such a sweet man. Do you just not want your brother to be happy? Because I simply can't believe you'd be that mean."

He wrapped his hand around the finger she'd shoved in his chest and invaded her personal space. The urge to kiss her, to touch her, was overwhelming. The woman was an addiction and he'd never even tasted her. He backed her up until she was against the door. All he wanted to do was take her right up against it, to shove her skirt up and sink deep inside her. "Of course I want him to be happy. I just worry he'll get his heart broken. He's... It doesn't fucking matter. He's my brother. I get to worry about him! And it's none of your business." And he could *not* make himself let go of her hand.

"Fine. If it's not my business, then this conversation is over!"

"It's not over!" It could never be over with her. He was pretty sure she literally just meant the conversation, but something about her tone made him panic, as if she meant they were over. Even if there was no 'they.'

She gave a half push against his chest. "It is over. And I'm not coming into work tomorrow. I'm taking a day off because if I have—"

Hell no. He wasn't letting her leave, wasn't letting her *not* come in tomorrow. Seeing her was the best part of his day. Even arguing with her was better than anything else. Feeling absolutely possessed, he crushed his mouth over hers. To his utter fucking surprise she leaned into him immediately, moaning into his mouth as her fingers dug into his shoulders. He plunged a hand into her short hair, cupping the back of her head in a tight grip. He'd wanted to taste her for so long and now he didn't want to let Lucy go.

Ever.

This woman owned him, had from practically the moment they'd hired her. It didn't matter that this was wrong on multiple levels. He couldn't get enough of her and now that he knew she wanted him back...

No, no, no. She should be shoving him back, telling him that he was an asshole and that she was going to file a sexual harassment charge against him. That was what she *should* do, he told himself. She was too good for him, far too sweet.

And his *assistant.* They shouldn't be doing this.

But when she moaned again and kissed him harder, completely melting against him, he lost his mind. How many times had he fantasized about doing this, about doing so much *more* than this?

Blindly reaching out, he locked his office door with his free hand and pulled back to look down at her, still cupping the back of her head.

Her dark hair was tousled and her lips slightly swollen, her dark eyes dilated with desire. When she touched her tongue to her bottom lip, tasting him on her own mouth, he didn't fight the groan that escaped. He could imagine her tongue stroking him everywhere, wished she had her mouth wrapped around his cock right now.

They both stared at each other, breathing hard, and even though he knew this was a mistake, he couldn't seem to make himself stop.

And not touching her wasn't an option. This woman pushed him to the very edge of his control. He wanted to protect her in a way he'd never imagined. He wanted to give her anything she wanted, to give her so much pleasure she never walked away from him.

Slowly, he went down onto his knees in front of her. He was going to taste all of her, feel her wetness on his tongue. He'd fantasized too many times what she'd taste like, how she'd sound as he gave her pleasure. She watched him, wide-eyed, her breathing growing more erratic.

"Tell me to stop," he growled, barely hanging onto his control. Once he put his mouth to her, once he got a taste of her, he wasn't stopping until she came against his tongue.

She shook her head, her expression slightly dazed.

He knew he should demand that she vocalize it, but fuck it. He was a selfish bastard. He wanted to taste her, wanted to show her how good things could be between them. He wasn't above tying her to him with sex, at least at first. He would just get her addicted to him.

Keeping his gaze pinned to hers he shoved her pencil skirt up to her hips to reveal bright red... He slid his hands up the back of her thighs and didn't stop until he cupped her smooth, bare ass. *Yep, thong.*

He groaned. His cock shoved insistently against his zipper but that would just have to wait.

"I've wondered what you wear underneath your clothes," he rasped out.

She still watched him, a mix of nerves and lust clear on her pretty face. "Really?" she whispered.

"All the fucking time," he growled. "I stroke myself off thinking about it, about *you.*"

Her shiny lips parted, her chest rising and falling, but she didn't say anything. Just watched him. He wanted to see her completely naked, to have her stretched out underneath him as he worshiped her entire body.

He wanted to see her lose every bit of her control and to stake his claim, to ruin her for any other man. Hell yeah, he wanted her so damn addicted to him that he was all she could think about. Because the truth was, *she* was all he could think about. He'd forced himself to keep his distance whenever he could, but there were times when he hadn't been able to stay away. He'd search her out, ask for stupid menial tasks just so he could talk to her, see her face to face.

Even though he wanted to thrust into her over and over and lose himself inside her, for now he'd settle for making her come against his tongue.

"You wet, baby?" he rasped out, his heart thundering against his ribs. She was so fucking gorgeous, all aroused and waiting to see what he did next.

Her eyes were a little glazed over, as if she couldn't believe they were doing this. Well, he couldn't either.

She nodded, her cheeks flushing pink as she licked her lips.

Still keeping his gaze on hers, he slowly pulled the front of her thong to the side before sliding his finger between her soft folds. Just a tease, a bare touch that made him shudder.

She was soaked.

He swallowed a rough groan. "Does arguing with me get you hot?"

"You get me hot," she breathed out, her words unsteady. Her fingers slid through his hair, her touch tentative.

It was exactly what he'd wanted to hear. Inhaling her sweet scent he leaned forward and swiped his tongue along her folds. Moaning, she jerked against his face and he lost it.

Grasping one of her ankles, he lifted her leg over his shoulder, spreading her open wider for him.

"Abram…" Her voice was nervous, unsteady.

"You want to stop, baby?" He hated to even ask, but he wanted her comfortable, for there to be no room for regret.

"No." But she still seemed nervous.

He sucked with words, had no idea how to reassure her. He just wanted to make her feel good. That, he knew he could do. Leaning forward again, he flicked his tongue over her clit and she let out the sweetest moan of pleasure.

He teased the sensitive nub again, adding more pressure even as he slid a finger inside her. "You're so tight," he moaned against her.

He imagined what she'd feel like wrapped around his cock, milking him until he was completely sated. Though for how he felt he didn't think he'd ever get enough of Lucy. Thoughts of her had been consuming him for months. She was his secret addiction. He hadn't been lying; he jerked off to thoughts of her more than he would admit.

Lucy gasped and rolled her hips again, her inner walls clenching around him as he added another finger into her tight body. She was biting her lower lip now, her cheeks flushed, eyes glowing with need.

Her fingers dug into his scalp as he continued teasing her clit, flicking his tongue against it over and over. The more pressure he added, the more she jerked against him, practically riding his face.

He wanted to lie flat on his back and let her do it from above, to completely bury his face in her sweet pussy.

"*Abram.*" Her body jerked and he knew she was going to come, could feel the way her inner walls convulsed faster and faster. "Oh..."

When her fingers dug into his scalp he savored the sweet bite of pain as she fell over the edge, her breathing out of control, her cries of pleasure music to his ears as she reached climax.

He didn't stop licking her until she gasped "Too much," the words coming out breathless.

Feeling almost drunk, he looked up to find her staring at him through heavy-lidded eyes. She looked as if she'd been thoroughly fucked, which she had, by his tongue. Too bad it hadn't been his cock yet. But it would soon. Tonight, if he had any say about it.

But not up against his office door. She deserved better than that. He wanted to take her back to his place, to completely worship her body, bring her orgasm after orgasm. Then he wanted to talk about their future, because he couldn't let her walk away after this.

They both jumped at the sound of a soft knocking coming from the outer office. "Hello? Mr. Ivanov?" a male voice called out.

"Oh God," Lucy rasped out, her expression morphing to one of horror. Her eyes widened as she slid her leg off his shoulder. Her legs wobbled and he set a hand on her hip to steady her, a rush of masculine pride roaring through him. He'd loved making her come against his tongue, loved that he'd made her unravel. Avoiding his gaze, she shoved her skirt down with trembling hands as he pushed to his feet.

He pulled out a handkerchief and wiped his face. His fingers smelled like Lucy and sex so he just shoved his hand in his pocket. He didn't want to lose that scent.

He also didn't want her to regret anything because he certainly didn't. "Lucy—"

She shook her head. "I don't want to talk about this here," she rushed out, her cheeks crimson. She quickly turned away from him, smoothing her hair down before she jerked the door open.

One of his drivers and another employee who worked in HR were standing in the doorway. *Fuck.* He couldn't chase after Lucy now, not when it was clear two employees needed to talk to him. He didn't want to embarrass her and he wasn't sure if they'd heard anything. From their expressions he didn't think so, but who the hell knew.

He nodded once at Kir. "I'll be down in twenty," he said.

The HR employee asked, "Got a few minutes?"

"Yeah." Even if all he wanted to do was chase after his very sexy assistant who was covertly trying to make her escape. She'd gone into Viktor's office but Abram knew that as soon as he stepped back into his own she'd be leaving for the night.

To escape him and what had happened here.

If she thought she could run from him, she was very much mistaken. Now that he'd tasted her come, felt her climax against his face, he didn't think he was ever letting her go.

* * *

Viktor wiped his damp palms against his pants as he headed up to Dominique's condo. He hadn't been this nervous in...

He'd never been this nervous. It was ridiculous.

She was on the second floor of a small, Mediterranean-style complex. It was in a good area and had decent security. Not good enough for her though. He'd never been particularly protective of anyone before. Well, other than his mother, but he'd been a child when she'd died. And of course Lucy.

But the protectiveness he felt for Dominique was very different. He wanted to put himself between her and anything that might ever threaten her. He wanted to make sure she never got hurt again. When he reached her door it swung open before he could knock.

As usual his heart rate kicked up at the sight of her. She had on a green and white summer dress that fell a little lower than mid-thigh. With her legs it was pretty much guaranteed that anything showing off all that skin looked good on her. She'd left her pale blonde hair down so that it fell in soft waves around her shoulders and face.

"I was waiting for you," she said, her light laugh just a little nervous. "Did you want to come in for a drink before we head out?"

He wanted to say yes, but shook his head. Viktor didn't want to know more about her, to see more of her life, because it would just show him what he couldn't have.

He was only here tonight because she wanted to talk about the contract. Okay, that was a lie—he wanted to spend time with her. But he knew that she was only here for one reason. So he wouldn't pretend otherwise. And going into her place and having a drink before they went out sounded like something people on dates did. This wasn't a date. "I wasn't sure where you would want to go so I chose a place on the beach. Cuban food, and mainly locals eat there."

"Sounds good." She grabbed her purse, which was more of a small pocketbook than anything, before shutting the door behind her.

"Don't you need to set your alarm?" he asked as she locked her door.

Her eyes widened slightly as she turned to him. "Ah...I don't have a system. Well, my place is wired for it. I just don't have a paid service right now."

He frowned as she fell in step beside him.

"What?"

He lifted a shoulder. It wasn't as if she was his. He had no say over her life. "Nothing. I brought a couple copies of the contract," he said. "If there's something you don't like we can fix it, but I think you'll be okay with it. You should still have an attorney look at it, regardless."

"I lied," she blurted as they reached the stairs. "I don't want to talk about the contract."

Ah, here it came. Keeping his expression neutral, he braced himself for what she was going to say. His brother had been right. Maybe she'd asked him out tonight to—

"I just wanted to spend time with you. As in...a date." She cringed, guilt flickering in her dark eyes. "I'm sorry. I should have just been honest with you."

He blinked in surprise, wondering when she'd drop the punch line, but he realized she was being serious. "You want to go on a date with me?"

She nodded, looking almost miserable. "I shouldn't have used the contract as an—"

"It's fine." His words came out more harshly than he'd intended. Viktor cleared his throat. All his muscles tightened as her words sank in. She wanted to go out with him. For no other reason than she wanted to spend time with him. "I would like to take you out as well." He inwardly cringed at how formal he sounded. But everything about this woman made him forget how to function.

Her cheeks flushed the sexiest shade of pink. "Okay, then. No contract talk tonight?"

"None."

"Good." She lightly curled her fingers around his upper arm and gave him a soft, almost shy smile that made him half desperate to kiss her. He could easily imagine her hands stroking over his naked body and had to shut that thought down. "I'm hungry. Let's get out of here."

He was hungry too, but not for food. Keeping that thought at bay, he nodded once. The feel of her fingers grazing him ever so lightly was heaven and hell.

This woman made him want too much.

That was a very dangerous thing. The last time he'd fallen for a woman he'd learned too late that everything they'd shared was a lie. That she'd felt nothing for him. The shame of that memory flared inside him now, nearly consuming him. It also reminded him why he only used escorts. There was never any question of where they stood.

But when he looked at the beautiful woman on his arm he knew that he wouldn't be able to simply walk away from Dominique, no matter how great the risk.

Even if she did have ulterior motives, a dark part of him didn't care if she used him. He'd let himself be used by her if it meant he got a taste of her in the bargain.

CHAPTER EIGHT

Dominique couldn't fight the jitters humming through her as Viktor opened the front door of the restaurant leading out into the parking lot. Dinner with him had been fun, even if he had seemed awkward at times. If anything, it endeared him even more to her.

He truly was nothing like she'd expected.

When he placed his big hand at the small of her back she could feel the heat of his touch straight to her skin. And she wondered what it would feel like to have him touching her bare skin. She'd been thinking about it all through dinner and questioning if she'd lost her mind. More than anything, she wondered if he'd be sensual, gentle...maybe a little rough.

"Thank you for dinner," she murmured. Her flat sandals crunched over the gravelly parking lot as they made their way to his SUV. She was glad that he hadn't had a driver tonight, that it was just them. She kept obsessing, wondering if he was going to kiss her—and really hoping he would. Everything about him screamed sex and power, and she really, *really* wanted to see what it would be like to lose herself with a man like Viktor.

He grunted a non-response before clearing his throat. "I'd like to take you out again. Tomorrow."

Yep, those butterflies were out of control in her stomach right about now. "I'd like that too," she said as they reached the passenger-side door.

Instead of opening the door for her, he gripped the handle and looked down at her, his body turned toward hers. She wondered what it would be like if he pressed her up against the vehicle and kissed her senseless, just took complete control. She squeezed her legs together at the thought. Everything about Viktor screamed power and control, and she found that she liked that. A lot. In college she'd dated a little, and when she hung out with her girlfriends they usually brought guys.

Now, the guys she'd dated or gone out with seemed like boys. There was nothing boyish about Viktor. He had a hard, dangerous edge to him that shouldn't fascinate her so much, but…she couldn't help herself.

When he reached out to cup her cheek, she sucked in a slight breath. His palm was callused and she liked the feel of it against her skin. There was nothing soft about this man. Her nipples beaded tightly against her bra at his simple touch.

His gaze fell to her mouth as he stroked a gentle thumb across her cheek. There was something intense about the moment as he looked down at her. When he looked at her like that she felt as if she was the only person who existed for him.

On instinct, she arched her body into his, erasing the space between them. He seemed to be keeping a wall up between them, but if he was going to kiss her, she wanted to feel him pressed up against her, feel that huge body on hers. And she really hoped he would take control. She might not know exactly what she wanted in a relationship or even sex, but deep down she thought that might be something she needed to be satisfied with a partner. For most of her life she'd towered over men, and while she was confident in who she was, she wanted a man who made her feel treasured and who could take complete control.

He murmured something in Russian, the words harsh sounding before he lowered his mouth to hers.

She closed her eyes as his lips barely touched hers—and cried out as a hard hand shoved into the middle of her back, sending her flying into Viktor. Her purse was ripped from her hand as she slammed into him. His back collided with the side mirror as her nose rammed against his chest. Tears stung her eyes from the abrupt impact.

She held onto him, trying to steady herself, but he grasped her upper arms and quickly shoved her behind him just as she heard the squeal of tires and flying gravel. Had someone been waiting in a car for this?

"Stay put," he ordered, pulling out a gun before racing to the back of the SUV.

Shock punched through her at the sight of the gun, but she swiped at the tears on her cheeks and stayed crouched by the front tire.

He let out a string of angry Russian words she was pretty sure were curses, before turning back to her. "He's gone. He had a getaway driver."

On trembling legs she pushed up from her crouch. Her nose felt sensitive but she was just glad she and Viktor were unharmed. "You carry a gun?" she blurted out even though yeah, it was pretty freaking obvious he did.

Ignoring her question, he tucked it under his shirt and out of sight. She probably shouldn't be surprised but it somehow took her off guard. That wasn't the thing she should be worrying about right now though. But she was feeling off balance in a big way. Trembles racked her body as she thought about what could have truly happened, how much worse things could have been. Someone could have stabbed or shot them.

Moving to her, he ran his hands up and down her arms, his gaze sweeping over her from head to foot in a purely clinical way. "Are you okay?"

"Yeah, I...we need to call the police. And I need to cancel my bank card immediately. Are you okay?"

He blinked, frowning at the question, as if she'd asked the most insane thing ever. He pulled out his phone. "Do you know your bank's number?"

"Yes... Crap, I've got to cancel my phone now too. God, that was insane. Did you get a look at who took my purse? Oh, maybe they have security footage here the cops can use."

Viktor simply nodded, scanning the parking lot, and opened the passenger door for her. "Get inside." The words came out like an order. "Ah, please," he added when she raised her eyebrows at his brusque tone. "I want to keep you safe."

The way he said those simple words did something strange to her insides. He said it as if he truly meant it. As if her safety was the most important thing to him.

She slid into the seat, and for some reason wasn't really surprised when he actually buckled her in. The way he just took charge sometimes made her melt. Heart still beating out of control, she started to dial her bank as he rounded the front of the vehicle.

To her surprise he pulled out another phone and made a call, speaking in Russian as she made her own phone calls. First she canceled her bank card and then reported her phone stolen. This was a huge pain in the ass but she was just glad they were okay. Once she was done, he was wrapping up his call as well. She handed him his phone as he started the engine.

"Wait, what about the police?"

He snorted, the sound laced with the slightest bit of derision. "I'm not calling the cops."

"Why not? I was just *mugged*." They needed to make a report.

"I want to get the locks changed on your condo tonight. I've already called someone and I'm having it taken care of immediately."

"My locks... Oh my God. They've got my address and my keys." At least she hadn't had any work keys in her purse. She'd just brought the basics tonight.

"What else did you have in there?" he asked, steering out of the parking lot.

She wanted to argue with him about not calling the police, but answered. "My phone and debit card, both of which are taken care of now. A little cash and some makeup stuff."

"No work stuff?"

"No."

"Okay. Good."

"Now why aren't you calling the police?"

"Because they won't be able to do a damn thing about tonight. Did you see the man who took your purse?" he asked, even though he had to know she hadn't seen a thing.

Biting her lip, she shook her head. "I didn't even get a glimpse of him." One moment she'd been almost kissing Viktor and the next someone had shoved her into him. "Where did he even come from?"

"He must have been waiting for us. There was someone waiting with him which means a team timed this perfectly, waiting until we were distracted." Viktor's voice was tight with barely concealed rage. "I should have kept you safer. I'm sorry."

There was so much self-recrimination in his voice it made her pause. "Viktor, it was just a random mugging. It's not your job to keep me safe. I'm just glad we're okay."

He seemed troubled. "I...don't necessarily know that it was random."

A new thread of fear slid through her veins. "What? Why would you think that?"

He glanced in the rearview mirror before switching lanes. "Mud was rubbed across the license plate, and the way it was almost choreographed..." He shook his head, his expression darkening. "I have a lot of enemies and you were out with me." Again, there was that note in his voice she didn't like.

"Some jerk stole my purse. It's no one's fault but his. And I can't imagine someone mugging me simply because

I was out with you. That doesn't even make sense." He had to see that.

But instead of agreeing with her, he just did that grunting thing and took the next turn.

Sighing, she leaned back against the seat, fighting the rush of nerves that had invaded her and didn't seem to be going away. Something so much worse could have happened tonight. What if her mugger had been carrying a weapon? She fought off a shudder, and to her surprise, Viktor reached out and squeezed her thigh, ever so lightly.

"I'm going to find out who did this." There was a blade-sharp edge to his voice that took her off guard, but she just nodded.

The truth was in his voice and part of her felt bad for her mugger. Because if a man like Viktor *did* find him... She was pretty sure he'd hurt the guy. And she didn't know what to think about that.

Didn't know what to think about anything lately. Viktor had completely knocked her world off its axis and she was only now coming to terms with the fact that she was insanely attracted to him. A man who most definitely had a shady history in business and was the son of a man she'd considered her enemy for a long time.

Even though she was worried about her stolen purse, she still couldn't help but wish that they'd gotten to follow through on that kiss. What would it have felt like to have Viktor's lips teasing hers and his body pressed up tight against hers?

She wasn't even sure what she'd like. Her sexual experiences consisted of kissing and what her mother would have called 'heavy petting.' All over the clothes.

After her mom had killed herself Dominique had retreated into herself, just working through college and barely even going out with friends the first couple years. The only people she'd even let into her life had been her extended family. Looking back, she realized that she'd been depressed. It had taken a long damn time to crawl out of her self-imposed prison. Not only that, she'd been afraid of sex for a long time. Her mom had been used sexually, had felt so ashamed that she'd killed herself. Even after Dominique had managed to start living again, she'd still shied away from sex.

So now she was a twenty-five-year-old virgin and for the first time she wondered if that would be an issue. The men she'd dated in the last few years had all been metrosexual types and more often than not the kind of men who used more beauty products than her. None of them had ever gotten her remotely hot enough to even consider sex. She'd go on a date or two and realize that nope, the guy wasn't for her. It wasn't like she was saving herself for marriage, but she wanted her first time to mean something, to be with someone who got her so turned on that she couldn't think straight—

"I promise I'll find who took your purse." Viktor's hard voice cut through her thoughts, his gaze on her intense as they idled at a stoplight.

"W-what...oh, okay. That's good." She stuttered over her words, embarrassed that she'd been so caught up in her own thoughts she hadn't been paying attention to anything else. It was clear he thought she was worried about her stupid purse when all she wanted to do was tell Viktor about her lack of experience.

But she wanted to wait to see if they even had a second date after this. That wasn't the kind of thing she could just blurt out. If things moved forward she'd definitely tell him. Especially if things got more heated between them.

And she really, really hoped that they did.

* * *

"Keep your eyes to yourself," Viktor growled out, careful to speak in Russian to Dimitri, the friend he'd asked to come over and change out Dominique's lock.

Viktor could have done it himself, but this particular friend had been a thief in another life and had the right tools and hardware on hand—because Dimitri now owned a string of hardware stores around Miami and in Homestead. Installing locks wasn't part of his normal job description but he was doing Viktor a favor.

Didn't mean he had to let the guy stare at Dominique. Not that he blamed him, but it still annoyed Viktor.

Dimitri just grinned and went back to installing the lock.

"Thank you again for doing this," Dominique said, standing close to Viktor as she watched Dimitri finish up.

"Thank Viktor, not me." Dimitri didn't look up as he worked.

Viktor's annoyance was somewhat appeased at his friend's words.

Dominique glanced up at Viktor then, her cheeks flushing slightly. Just the sight of her like that made him think of what she'd look like after sex—and during sex. And he'd had way too many fantasies in the past few days about that.

"Thank you," she murmured, sliding her hand around his upper arm the same way she'd done at the beginning of the evening. Her fingers rested gently against his skin, her hold light.

He loved the way she touched him and he knew it was because she wanted to. Not because she was paid to. Or...he assumed she wanted to. That doubt still lingered in the back of his head, wondering if she was somehow using him.

He quickly shelved the thought, not wanting his past bullshit to color the time he spent with her. If she was using him, he'd deal with it later.

Right now he wanted to kick his own ass for not being able to protect Dominique tonight. Someone—more than one person—had worked very carefully to make sure they were able to grab her purse and flee with a backup driver for a supposedly simple mugging. Everything about what happened felt off and he was pissed that he'd let his guard down.

As Dimitri worked, he gently pulled Dominique down the exterior walkway, wanting to give them a little more privacy. Her complex had been very quiet tonight, or at least her building and floor. He'd only seen one neighbor arrive since they'd been back.

"What's wrong?" she asked, still holding onto his arm as she turned her body toward his.

With her so close to him, her breasts brushing against his arm as she shifted, it took serious effort to think. He cleared his throat. "I'm going to give you a phone to keep, just overnight, until you can get a new one tomorrow. I don't like the thought of you not having a way to contact anyone and I'm guessing you don't have a landline." Almost no one did anymore.

Her expression softened and she brushed a hand down his chest, just briefly touching him. "I didn't even think of that. Thank you."

All his muscles pulled taut at her touch. It was as if she was trying to make him crazy with need. "I'm also going to have someone watch your condo. Just tonight."

She blinked in confusion, then shook her head. "That's really sweet, but it's not necessary."

"Look... I don't know if the mugging tonight was random or not. I don't like how it happened." He didn't like telling her this much—didn't want her to know what kind of man he was, how many enemies he had. But he wouldn't risk her safety for anything. "I've made a lot of enemies over the years. People who don't like their businesses getting bought out. I've never had a..." He paused, looking for the right word. He'd never had a woman in his life before, and even if they weren't in a relationship she *meant* something to him. "You and I have been potentially seen together at multiple places. If someone thinks you're important to me it's not out of the realm of possibility that they might target you to get to me."

She blinked at him again. "I...that seems a little crazy."

"Then you can humor me."

Her eyes narrowed slightly. "That sounds a little bit like an order."

He lifted a shoulder. "I'm having someone watch the place whether you like it or not." Yeah, he knew that was high-handed but he didn't care. "I could lie and tell you I wasn't, but I'm not going to lie to you."

"You are...frustrating."

"I've been called worse," he said dryly.

She snorted, the sound adorable. "Fine."

Consumed with the need to touch her, he slid his hands down to her hips, pulling her close to him. There was no way to hide his erection from her and he didn't want to. She should have no doubt how she affected him. "I want to kiss you right now," he murmured.

Her eyes were dilated and her breathing grew erratic at his words. She set her hands on his chest. "Why don't you?" Her voice was a whisper.

"Because when I do, I don't want an audience." His employee was waiting at the end of the hallway, watching Dominique's place. Not to mention Dimitri was a few doors down and there were any number of nosy neighbors potentially watching.

She hitched in a breath at his words, her gaze falling to his mouth.

"Can I take you to lunch tomorrow?" He kept his voice low, somehow resisting the urge to lean down and claim her mouth.

She nodded, that almost dazed look back as she met his gaze. "I'd like that."

Yeah, he would too. Way too much. Pushing against his own self-control, he reached up and cupped her cheek, slowly slid his thumb over her full bottom lip. What he wouldn't give to kiss her right now.

Just the thought was tempting, but he hadn't been lying. He didn't want anyone to see him kissing her. Didn't want anyone to hear her moans of pleasure, no matter how small. She made him feel ridiculously possessive and those sounds were just for him.

He was moving into unknown territory with her but he knew that once they crossed the line into a physical relationship he was going to consider her his.

CHAPTER NINE

"You staying in the building for lunch, or heading out?" At the sound of Lizzy's voice, Dominique looked up from her computer.

"Ah…" She glanced at her cell phone, surprised it was lunch already. She'd been working nonstop all morning. "I've got to grab a new phone at lunch. I'm just going to walk down to the store."

Lizzy frowned as she sat on the edge of Dominique's desk—as per usual for her. Today she had on flip-flops, jeans and a T-shirt that said 'Unicorns love bad girls' with a picture of a unicorn wearing a biker jacket under the text. "What happened to your phone?"

Dominique didn't want to lie to her friend, even if she still felt weird about not calling the police. "It was stolen. I was actually mugged last night. My purse was taken and my phone was in it."

Lizzy's eyes widened. "Are you okay?"

She nodded. "Yeah, annoyed but fine."

"Still, that sucks. Where did it happen?"

"Outside a restaurant. I was with…Viktor when this guy just snatched it."

"I'm surprised he didn't kill the guy. What did the cops say?"

Dominique bit her bottom lip. "He didn't call them. Said they couldn't do anything about it and then he got someone to change my locks since my license and keys were in my purse."

Lizzy's expression morphed to one of something that looked a lot like respect. "Good for Ivanov."

"You don't think it's weird he didn't want to call the cops?"

Her friend lifted a shoulder. "Maybe. I don't know. It depends on a lot of things and I don't know how he feels about cops in general. But I can guess. If you tell me what restaurant it happened at I might be able to find out more information for you. I could hack into some CCTVs if you want." She rubbed her hands together, looking way too excited and a little scary.

"If you start cackling like some sort of evil villain, I'm out of here. And I'm not going to tell you where it was. I'm not supporting your hacking habit."

"I'll find out on my own, you know."

Dominique lifted a shoulder, fighting a smile. "If you have extra time to figure it out, go for it. It was just a stupid mugging and everything is thankfully replaceable." She was really glad Viktor'd had her locks changed though. She'd been able to sleep easier last night.

Lizzy just grinned. "Fine... So, have you talked to Raegan this morning?"

"Yeah, she texted me that she and the sexy cop are a thing again." Dominique wasn't sure what to think about that, considering the guy had ghosted on Raegan for a few days. But if the man made Raegan happy, that was what mattered.

"He's a good guy. Relationship challenged, that's for sure."

Dominique laughed. "What guy isn't?" Not that she really had a leg to stand on—she'd never even been in a serious relationship either. "Listen, I've gotta head out if I want to beat the rush. Your man should just be getting off his conference call." She glanced at the phone, saw Porter's light still on. "Or he will be in a minute or two."

Lizzy's expression went pure wicked as she headed for the adjoining door. "If getting your phone takes your whole lunch break, just extend your lunch so you get to eat. I'll tell Porter you'll be longer than usual." Without waiting for a response she opened the door and ducked inside. The lock snicked into place behind Lizzy.

At that, Dominique grabbed her purse and practically raced out of there. It was pretty rare that Lizzy came down to their floor during work hours and Dominique didn't want to stick around for whatever was about to happen.

The elevator made four stops before finally reaching the lobby. It was weird not having her phone. She felt almost naked without it. Even though she'd had her phone locked she'd still changed all her passwords this morning too. Something she should have thought about last night, but she'd been consumed with thoughts of Viktor.

She blinked when she saw him standing in the lobby near one of the huge pillars, talking to Harrison Caldwell, of all people. He was one of the owners. His father had founded Red Stone, but since semi-retiring recently he'd left his three sons in charge of everything. It didn't matter that Porter was Harrison's brother—Dominique still felt nervous around him. The man had an edge to him. Not that Viktor was any less scary, but...she wasn't afraid of Viktor.

As if he sensed her, Viktor turned and pinned her with those icy blue eyes. Though his look was anything but cold. A blast of heat radiated off him, the hunger in his eyes clear as his gaze swept her over from head to toe.

Her surroundings melted away as she headed toward him. She'd called him early this morning and rescheduled their lunch so maybe he was here to see Harrison. Whatever the reason, she didn't care. She was glad she'd run into him, regardless. Her heart rate was out of control as she drank in the sight of him. He had on dark pants, a button-down shirt, a custom-cut jacket and no tie. She loved the look on him.

"Hey," she murmured as she reached him.

His mouth curved up ever so slightly and she wondered if that was his version of a smile. Whatever it was, she liked it. A lot. Seriously, how had this happened? How had she started to fall for Viktor Ivanov so dang fast?

"You look beautiful," he said quietly.

The simple words took her off guard and pleased her at the same time. She started to respond when Harrison Caldwell—whose presence she'd completely forgotten about—cleared his throat.

"I've gotta go," he said, nodding once at her before focusing on Viktor. "We'll talk later."

Viktor simply nodded before turning back to her. "I thought I'd walk with you to the phone store. Then lunch if you have time."

She was irrationally pleased he'd decided to meet her here. "I think I'll have time. I just saw on Twitter that one of my favorite food trucks is supposed to be a couple blocks from here for the next few hours."

"Food trucks have Twitter accounts?" He sounded dubious.

Laughing, she linked her arm through his. "Everyone does. Even you."

"No, some of my *companies* do... Lucy hired a team of people to head up our social media accounts. I've never looked at them."

"Yeah, I can't see you actually tweeting. Or using Snapchat." She laughed when he just gave her a blank look. "You sure you don't mind coming with me? I might not even be able to sneak in a lunch break if they're too busy."

"You will be able to." He sounded ridiculously confident about that as they reached one of the big glass doors.

A rush of Florida heat rolled over them as they stepped outside. She savored the warmth after being cooped up inside all morning in the air-conditioned space, and slid off her light cardigan sweater. "Why does that sound as if you know that for a fact?"

"I know the owner of this particular store. I made a call."

"Viktor..." She trailed off when he looked down at her, pinning her with such a heated look she felt it all the way to her core. A Florida summer had nothing on him. "What?"

"I like it when you say my name." The words were a sexy growl.

She felt her cheeks flush and couldn't blame it on the weather. Viktor had gotten under her skin, and she had no idea if she was ready for a man like this because she was pretty sure he was way out of her league. Deep down she wondered if he was going to freak out when she told him about her lack of experience. Part of her didn't want to tell him, but she was beginning to really trust Viktor— which scared her too.

* * *

"So, it's good information right?" his contact asked.

He tried to keep his tone disinterested, but this was gold and the man had to know it. "Very good." Last night he'd received pictures of the blonde woman and Viktor out at a restaurant and it had looked like a date. "How'd you get the pictures without him seeing you?"

There was a short pause, then, "Because I'm very good at being invisible."

"You're sure?"

"Yes. It was easy to follow him. I placed a tracker on his SUV last night so I didn't need him in my line of sight. I just followed the tracker."

"Have you removed the tracker?" He didn't want Viktor to know anyone was targeting him. Not yet. Not until it was too late for the fucker to do anything about it.

"Of course," the man snapped. "Did you get what you needed from her purse?"

"Yes." After he'd received the location of Viktor and the woman last night he'd sent a well-trained team of two to mug her.

He'd needed it to seem random but also have a team good enough to surprise Viktor. The circumstances had been perfect for the mugging. Viktor hadn't had his driver and he'd been wrapped up in that whore. Unfortunately, now Viktor seemed to have someone watching the woman's place. That seemed a bit paranoid but also confirmed what he'd needed to know—Viktor cared for the woman.

"I overheard Lucy talking to someone on the phone yesterday. I think it was about this Dominique Castle. Lucy was confirming with someone that she works for Red Stone Security," he said.

A thread of alarm worked its way through his system. "Hmm, that could be a problem."

"Why? It's not like you're going to hurt the woman, right?"

The owner of Red Stone Security and his sons weren't the kind of people you messed with. Then again, neither was Viktor. He ignored the question. The woman might get hurt, she might not—but he was pretty certain she would die too. "Maybe it won't be a problem. She is important to Ivanov though, that much I'm sure of. I know for a fact he had someone change her locks last night."

"How do you know that?"

"Because I had someone go to her condo complex last night. She's a beautiful woman," he said, looking at her picture again. "It'll be a shame to waste all that beauty. Keep me updated with anything else. Your payment is on the way." He hung up before the man could respond and traced a finger over Dominique Castle's face.

What kind of woman got involved with a man like Ivanov, he wondered. She'd have to be a whore. No doubt about it. She'd get what she deserved too.

* * *

Viktor pulled out his phone as he left one of the hotels he and Abram had recently bought. This was one they wouldn't keep, but would reorganize, get it running right again, then sell for a profit. His driver was waiting outside, the SUV idling as he approached. Viktor waved him off from getting out to open his door and slid into the back seat, calling Abram as Kir pulled away.

"Hey, I'm calling it a day." Normally he'd work another two or three hours but he wanted to see Dominique and she was free tonight. It amazed him that someone like her wanted to go out on a date with him, but he was determined not to fuck things up. He might not know anything about relationships, but he would learn. For her.

"Me too. I'm going to check on Lucy. I'm worried about her." There was an odd note in Abram's voice.

"She's sick. It happens. But...I think it's a good idea." Not that his brother was asking him. Because Abram wouldn't ask for anyone's opinion when it came to Lucy.

"Look, I want to hire a new assistant for me as soon as possible. We can start looking next week."

"Any reason for the rush?" Viktor thought he knew, but didn't want to assume.

His brother cleared his throat. "I don't think Lucy should be working under me anymore, for personal reasons. I want to...be with her. She can't work for me if that's going to happen."

"You finally tell her how you feel?" Viktor had been trying to ignore the chemistry between them but it was so damn obvious.

Abram cleared his throat again. "Sort of."

"We'll talk to HR, make sure—"

"I've already taken care of everything. No matter what happens between us she'll have job security. And we're giving her another fucking raise." He said the last part as if he thought Viktor might argue.

"Agreed. Look…how serious are you about her?" He glanced at his driver, who didn't seem to be paying attention, but he never underestimated anyone. He'd had the same driver for years, until recently when he'd promoted Lyosha to a different position.

"Very."

Good. "I heard her talking to a friend about a Bulgari necklace she said would be her Christmas present to herself one day—"

"I bought it a month ago."

His eyebrows shot up. "Shit, you are serious."

Abram just snorted. "You going out with Dominique tonight?"

Something in his brother's tone annoyed him. He gritted his teeth. "Yes."

"All right. Just…be careful. I called Lyosha, told him to head up an extra security team tonight. They're going to tail you, subtly. She won't know about it, but I want you to have some backup just in case. I don't like that mugging."

Viktor scrubbed a hand over his face. He didn't want to say too much in front of his driver, but he didn't like the way the mugging had gone down either. A two-man team for a simple snatch and grab? What he hadn't told Dominique was that he'd gone to the owner of the restaurant later that night and it turned out all their security cameras had been tampered with right around the time he'd arrived with Dominique.

Which meant someone could have followed him. He'd checked his vehicle for trackers and found nothing, but that didn't mean shit. Someone could have followed him or tracked him another way.

He'd left his life of crime behind but that didn't mean he didn't have enemies. And he didn't think for a second that she'd been the real target. This felt like a message to him. "I don't either," he finally said.

"What if she's involved? Maybe the whole thing was a setup." Abram's voice was tight, agitated.

"To what end?" He didn't believe it, regardless. Dominique had been shaken last night. Unless she was the best actress in the damn world, no, he didn't think she was involved with her own mugging.

"I don't know yet," Abram grumbled.

Viktor hid an exasperated sigh. "Why don't you quit worrying about me and worry about yourself?"

"You're my brother."

"I know." The truth was, he worried about Abram too. All the damn time. He was the only family Viktor had. "Let me know how Lucy is, if she needs anything."

Abram just grunted and hung up.

Shaking his head, Viktor tucked his phone into his pocket. He'd be seeing Dominique in less than an hour and the anticipation humming through him was like a live thing. She'd been on his mind all day, consuming him.

After she'd picked up a new phone today they'd grabbed lunch at a food truck and eaten at a nearby park. While he'd been vigilant about their surroundings, he'd realized that he'd been relaxed with her, unlike how he felt with most people. But it was as if she didn't *want* anything from him other than his company. Hell, she wouldn't even take the house. He'd tried to bring it up once but she'd shut him down fast.

It was clear she still hadn't made a decision about it, and that was fine with him. The longer it took her to figure out what she wanted, the longer he still had a reason to contact her. Not that he seemed to need one other than to simply ask her out.

He wanted more than just dating though. He didn't care if it was too soon—he couldn't just do casual. Not with a woman like her. He'd had casual sex, sex he paid for. He wanted something real. Even if he wasn't sure he deserved it.

The only problem was, he knew shit about relationships and women. He didn't want to come off too strong, but once they crossed a certain line, he knew he wouldn't let her go. He just hoped she was ready for him.

CHAPTER TEN

Feeling a little bit possessed, Abram pounded his fist against Lucy's front door again. He knew she was in there; had seen a light flip on about ten seconds ago. And he knew he was acting like a psycho. He just didn't care.

She lived on a quiet cul-de-sac with beach-cottage-style homes, some two-story but mostly one-story houses. A next-door neighbor stepped out from his front door, eyed Abram with suspicion. The guy was good-looking too, probably in his early thirties.

Shirtless and tanned, he glared at Abram. "You need something?" the man asked, his tone brusque.

"I'm here to see Lucy." He forced himself to remain civil even if it wasn't this guy's business who the hell he was. Still...he was glad Lucy had neighbors who cared enough to look out for her.

The man crossed his arms over his chest and leaned against the railing of the front porch. "Don't think she's home."

Before he could respond, Abram heard the click of the lock opening. Lucy jerked the door open, her expression unreadable as she watched him. She stepped out onto the porch and smiled at her neighbor. Some irrational part of Abram was jealous that the guy got to see her smile. He wanted all of that sweetness reserved for him, not some dick.

"Hey Leo, everything's good over here. This is just a friend. I asked him to stop by to help me with my...computer."

"You sure?" The neighbor's gaze flicked to Abram, clearly not trusting him.

"Yeah, I promise. Tell Maria I'll be bringing over that dish she left a little later this evening."

The man nodded, still not moving from his sentry position.

Lucy grabbed Abram's upper arm and practically dragged him inside, shutting and locking the door behind him. "What are you doing here?" She dropped her arm and placed both hands on her hips as she glared up at him.

"You're not sick." He swept his gaze over her, surprised to see her looking so casual, though he knew he shouldn't be. She was at home, not work or a function. She had on skimpy beach shorts that showed a whole lot of skin, a tank top and the straps of a blue and white bikini tied behind her neck. She'd once told him that she had a small pool in her backyard so he guessed she'd been using it.

She crossed her arms over her chest. "So what? I needed a sick day, so I took it. And you showing up here to check on me is completely inappropriate."

"As inappropriate as me eating your pussy at work?"

Her cheeks went bright pink. She opened her mouth but nothing came out as she stared up at him. Everything about her was adorable, right down to her painted cherry red toenails.

He was glad she wasn't talking because there were some things he needed to say and if he didn't get them out all at once he wasn't sure he ever would. "We're hiring someone new as soon as possible to be my assistant. You'll work directly under Viktor when that happens. I don't want there to be an imbalance of power between us and I can see how it could happen if I'm your boss—though to be fair, you boss me around a lot."

She let out a shaky laugh and he could see some of the tension leaving her shoulders. That had to be a good thing so he barreled on.

"I want to be with you. I want...you to be my girl-friend." Even saying that out loud was too strange. "Which is a dumb, fucking word. But I want to start something real with you and I know that can't happen unless there's a division between us at work." When she watched him with those big dark eyes, not saying any-thing, he started to panic. "Say something," he de-manded—okay, snarled.

Instead of being taken off guard, like any one of his employees would have been, she rolled her eyes. "Jeez, Abram. You've just shown up and dropped a lot on me. Can we sit down and talk?" She motioned to the attached living room.

He didn't want to fucking talk, but he did as she asked. When she sat on the long, white tufted couch he sat next to her, crowding her personal space. He'd been going crazy all day without seeing her, wondering if she was go-ing to quit because of what happened between them.

Thankfully she didn't seem to mind how close he was to her.

"I'm sorry I called in today. I felt really awkward about...what we did." Her cheeks flushed again and he had to restrain himself from reaching out and touching her. "I know it was pretty weak, but I called in sick so I could think."

"What's there to think about?" He'd just laid himself on the line, made himself completely vulnerable. The very idea of doing that for anyone else made his skin crawl. Not that doing it for her was much easier. If she shot him down... He swallowed hard. He hadn't thought that far ahead.

She clasped her hands together in her lap, her back ramrod straight. Even in her beach clothes she looked every inch the princess. "Well...us. I mean, you're my boss and—"

"I won't be your boss soon. And I've had HR and legal draw up papers so that no matter what happens between us, your job will never be affected. You will always have job security, no matter what." He didn't tell her that he wasn't letting her go, that he planned on convincing her to take a chance on forever with him. Even he knew it was too soon to say that out loud.

Her pretty lips parted, her expression softening. "You did all that?"

"Yes. And..." He reached into his jacket pocket and pulled out the long box he'd kept in his office for the last month. He handed it to her, not sure what to say. The thing had been burning a hole in his desk so he'd shoved it in his safe until today.

He'd overheard her conversation with a friend when she'd been on lunch break, talking about how once she'd gotten her retirement accounts maxed out for the next five years in a row, this was going to be her Christmas present to herself. Well fuck that. He was going to give it to her now. He wanted to give her the whole damn world, anything she wanted.

Her eyebrows raised slightly as she started to open the box. She let out a gasp when she saw the gold roped necklace inside. She ran her fingers over the thick chain almost reverently. "Abram, this is beautiful... Oh my God, no." She handed it back to him, her hand trembling even as she looked at the beautiful necklace. "I can't take this. It's over eight thousand dollars." She whispered the last part as if he'd committed a sin.

It was more like twelve grand because he'd had diamonds added to it, but he didn't correct her. "Who cares?"

She blinked. "It's too much. Way too much. And we're not even... What are we?" She linked her fingers together again in her lap.

"I told you what I want. What do you want?"

"You. Since the moment we met."

Relief slammed through him and without thinking he pulled her into his lap. She let out a squeak of surprise and then her cheeks flushed that sexy-as-fuck shade of pink again when she shifted over his erection.

"That's because of you," he murmured. He'd been walking around with a hard on for months because of her.

Sitting sideways in his lap, she turned more to face him, placing her gentle hands on his shoulders. He'd never thought to fall for anyone, but definitely not someone as delicate-looking as Lucy. He'd learned early on that she might look fragile, but she was a force of nature. He adored everything about her.

"So you and I...will be exclusive?" She sounded almost unsure about that.

He snorted. "I've been exclusive to you since we hired you." Because the thought of being with anyone else had been impossible. After he'd met Lucy, gotten to know the sweet woman who'd completely stolen his heart, everyone else paled in comparison.

Her lips parted slightly. "But I saw... I saw a jewelry box in your desk drawer a month ago. Just like that one. I thought maybe you were seeing someone..." She trailed off and for the first time since he'd known her, he could see true vulnerability in her dark eyes.

Without looking at it, he clasped it, slid it into her lap. "This is the *same* one. I bought this for you. I've never bought jewelry for another woman. Ever." He'd never even thought to. He'd had bed partners, that was it. No one he wanted to spend time with outside of the bedroom. Until sweet, sexy Lucy who'd become a bright light in his life.

"Oh." She bit her bottom lip, still looking unsure.

It drove him crazy. "What?"

"Nothing, just trying to wrap my head around all this. I've been into you since we met and I don't know, I tried to convince myself it was a stupid crush. Then when I saw that necklace I was...insanely jealous. Which I feel stupid admitting. It was gone the next day from your drawer so I assumed you'd given it to someone."

He decided not to tell her that he found her jealousy hot, but he liked knowing she gave a shit. "Is that why you've been frustrated with me the last month?"

"No. Maybe...yes."

He opened the box and lifted out the piece of jewelry, clasped it around her neck. "I want to fu—make love to you with just this on." It was totally barbaric but he wanted to claim her while she wore something he'd given her. Like he'd marked her.

She made a soft little moan and shifted in his lap, her eyes going heavy-lidded.

"You like the idea of that?" He knew he should offer to take her out to dinner, to do things a normal couple would do. But the need to be inside her, to claim her, was overwhelming.

Her breathing grew shallower as she lifted a hand to the necklace, gently ran her fingers along it. "This is too much," she whispered, but there was no conviction in her voice.

"That's not an answer, baby. You like the idea of me taking you wearing just this?" He leaned down, nipped her earlobe between his teeth. "Maybe fucking you from behind in front of a mirror so you can see us? See how sexy you look when I make you come?" He wanted to do more than just fuck, but the way Lucy reacted to his words told him she *liked* the way he was talking to her.

She clutched onto his shoulders, her breathing erratic as he scraped his teeth along the column of her neck. "There's a big mirror in my guest bedroom," she whispered again, her voice shaky.

The statement ricocheted through him, making him jerk against her. He pulled back slightly so he could see her face. "You want…" For some reason he couldn't finish the thought. Being here with her now was too surreal. In no reality did he end up with a woman like Lucy but here they were.

Her lips curved up into a mischievous grin as she slid off his lap. He made a move to pull her back but she dodged his hands and stripped off her tank top before turning away from him. Even the sight of her bare back got him insanely hot.

He was on his feet in a millisecond, following after her as she tugged the strings to her bathing suit free, letting her top fall to the ground as she headed down a brightly painted hallway.

All he could focus on was her back and the soft curve of her hips as she pushed open a door into a dimly lit bedroom. Sheer curtains were pulled together over the single window, letting in some of the waning early evening light. He leaned against the doorframe, fascinated with her, as she shimmied out of her shorts and bikini bottom without looking at him.

Her breasts weren't large, enough to fill his hands, and though she was petite her hips were full and perfect. Everything about her was perfect.

"Will this do?" Her sexy voice brought his gaze back up to hers.

He realized he'd been staring at the juncture between her thighs—the little bit of hair covering her mound. He'd been remembering how she tasted, how she'd felt as she'd come against his face and fingers. She'd pointed to the huge wood-framed mirror propped up behind a daybed with all sorts of frilly female stuff on it and around it. The room had a sort of Parisian theme to it. Something he most definitely didn't care about.

Keeping his gaze pinned to hers, he shoved away from the doorframe and slid his jacket off. She watched him carefully, her eyes wide and her body language just a little bit nervous, if the tremble that shuddered through her was any indication.

Moving slowly, he let her watch his every move, his hands going to his belt buckle. She sucked in a breath as she tracked his actions. When he was fully naked he grabbed a condom from his pants before stalking toward her. The most primal part of him liked it when she backed up to the daybed, her breathing raspy and unsteady.

There was nowhere for her to go, not that he thought she actually wanted to be anywhere but here. Her pale brown nipples were beaded tightly and he wanted to taste them, to taste all of her again.

Yesterday hadn't taken off any of the edge from the need to have her. It had only stoked the wildfire burning inside him. When he reached her, his cock jutted up between them, pressing against her belly.

She sucked in a breath as she looked down between their bodies, and to his pleasure, she grasped his hard length, a smile on her face. "You really are big all over," she murmured, more to herself than him.

Seeing the anticipation on her expression, the way her dark eyes went heavy-lidded as she stroked him once, made him groan as much as the feel of her fingers wrapped tightly around his cock did.

Even though he could easily come in her hand, he placed his over her smaller one. There was no way that was happening this first time. He would be inside her when he did. And she would most definitely come first.

When she looked up at him, he lowered his mouth to hers. Instead of crushing his lips against hers, which was what his body was demanding, his instinct said to take things slower with her.

At least this first time. He'd already made her come up against his office door; now he wanted to savor her, make sure she remembered their first time together.

The first time of many, if things went the way he hoped.

She slid her hands up his bare chest, her fingers digging into his pecs as he pushed her back onto the daybed. The thing was way too small but it would do for now.

He didn't know where to start now that he had her stretched out before him.

"Fuck, you're gorgeous," he rasped out as he straddled her on the narrow bed. It dipped under his weight, making her giggle.

The light sound eased something in his chest.

"What happened to...taking me from behind?" she whispered, watching him carefully, her eyes slightly dilated.

He noticed she didn't say the word fuck and found that insanely adorable. "We'll get there." He dipped his head to one of her breasts, sucked on her already hard nipple.

Moaning, she arched her back, sliding her fingers through his short hair even as she wrapped her legs around his waist, plastering herself to him. His cock was thick and heavy between them. The way she enveloped herself around him made all those possessive instincts he hadn't known he even *had* flare to life.

"Abram." His name sounded like a prayer on her lips and all he'd done was tease her nipple.

He bit down gently on the hard bud and she squirmed under him, her fingers now digging into his back.

Yeah, he could get used to hearing her say his name; wanted her to say it as he thrust inside her.

He reached between their bodies and cupped her mound even as he moved to her other breast, swiping his tongue around her nipple. He slid a finger between her slick folds, making her moan even louder as she rolled her hips against him.

His cock ached, begging to be inside her, but he needed to work her up a little more. Lifting his head from her breast, he crushed his mouth to hers.

She twined her tongue with his, just as hungry for him as he was for her. He could feel it in her every movement and hear it in every little gasp she made. When she gave his bottom lip a playful nip, lightly scraping her finger-nails down his back, his balls pulled up even tighter.

Though he wanted to keep kissing her, teasing her, he wanted her to come even more. This first time would take the edge off.

Pulling back from her, he stared down at her for a long moment. Her breasts rose and fell as she watched him, her dark eyes filled with hunger. When she reached for his cock, he grasped her wrist and pulled her up to a sitting position.

"On your knees. Face the mirror." He barely managed to get the words out, to keep a grasp on his control.

She did as he said, her movements unsteady and a little jerky. He liked that she was as affected as him. When she met his gaze in the mirror, he swore his heart stopped for a moment.

Her short, dark hair wasn't neat like it usually was, but mussed. Her lips were slightly swollen, and the look in her eyes was more than just lust. She looked like she needed him. Maybe as much as he needed her.

Moving in behind her, he took a moment to appreciate the differences in their bodies. She was so petite and slender, but with a steel backbone. He wasn't worried about hurting her, knew he could never do that.

He ran his hands down her sides, hated how callused his hands were, but she didn't seem to mind. She shuddered, holding onto the vintage metal frame of the daybed as she spread her legs just a little wider.

Even her pose, the way she was bent forward, waiting for him, made his breath catch. He was never letting her go.

He'd felt how slick she was but he still reached between her legs from behind, groaned at the feel of her. "You're so wet."

"I'm wet all the time for you." Her words came out low as she watched him in the mirror, her fingers clutching the frame. "You make me crazy at work and I *still* get turned on by it."

"Good." Because he got turned on by her all the damn time. Didn't matter what she seemed to be doing. He quickly rolled on a condom before guiding his cock to her entrance.

Soon, he planned to be inside her bare, with nothing between the two of them as he emptied himself inside her.

He didn't push inside her just yet though. Reaching around, he cupped both her breasts, teasing both her nipples with his thumbs as he watched her expression.

She sucked in a breath, pleasure playing across her expression as her head fell back against his chest. He loved seeing her like this, open to him.

And all his.

He worked her up until she was squirming and pushing her ass back against him, silently demanding he do something.

Without pause he thrust into her in one long push.

"Abram." She froze for a moment, her breathing shallow as she adjusted to his size.

He felt her inner walls tightening around him, already milking him. She was so damn tight and yeah, he was big. Nothing to be done about that. He buried his face against her neck, inhaled her sweet scent as he reached around and found her pulsing clit.

She needed to come, and fast. Because his control was slipping. Lucy'd had him on edge for months. Now that he was inside her, he knew he wasn't going to last long. Not this first time.

When he slid a finger over her clit, she moaned and jerked back against him. At the same time he felt her clench around him even tighter.

Using her body's cues, he stroked her clit, increasing the pressure the louder she moaned until he knew she was close.

"Oh God, oh…" She jerked against him as she rolled into climax.

He began thrusting inside her and she cried out even louder, her inner walls rippling around him as she found her release. He couldn't watch her in the mirror anymore as his own orgasm built and crested as months of need for her slammed through him.

He wasn't sure how long he thrust into her but his orgasm seemed to go on forever as he lost himself inside her.

When he looked at her in the mirror again, the satisfied expression on her face made him do a mental fist pump. It was the most beautiful thing he'd ever seen. And he'd put it there.

"We could have been doing this for months now," she murmured, giving him the most sensual look in the mirror.

He nipped her shoulder gently. "I think we should make up for lost time, then."

CHAPTER ELEVEN

"**I** can't even pretend I'm not impressed by this." Dominique looked around the empty five-star restaurant before focusing on Viktor again, her expression warm.

He'd never been on the receiving end of such raw openness before. Viktor would be lying if he said he wasn't glad she was impressed. He'd do fucking cartwheels if it made her happy. Anything to see Dominique smile.

He cleared his throat. "With the place under renovation I thought it would be nice for just the two of us to come here." He and Abram had shut down one of the hotels they'd recently purchased to renovate a good chunk of the place. But the restaurant right on the Atlantic was one of the only parts of the hotel that didn't need *any* work. So he'd brought in the chef—one of the few employees he planned to keep on staff while he restructured—to impress Dominique tonight.

He'd never cared about impressing anyone before. Even when he was younger, he'd just cared about people respecting and yes, fearing him. With Dominique... She brought out a completely different side to him. He was still adjusting to that.

"I'm glad you like it," he murmured, reaching across the linen-covered tabletop to slide his hand over hers.

Her cheeks flushed and he found himself getting hard. Again. She had an innocent quality to her that surprised him. Even more, he was surprised he liked it. When he'd had Abram run her information, when he was still wondering who she was and why she hated him, his brother hadn't found a record of any serious boyfriends.

There was no way a woman like Dominique could be a virgin, but he guessed she didn't have much experience. Which, yeah, he liked the thought of that too. But he didn't care how many guys she'd been with. That shit wasn't important. The only thing he cared about was locking her down now. Convincing her that they might have a shot at something real. The only problem was…he wasn't sure he could give her the kind of sexual experience she deserved. His only experience was with women he'd paid. Dominique would know nothing about that. The truth was, he knew it would disgust her. Which was why he had to tell her.

She was an absolute knockout but it was more than that. She was simply…sweet. He didn't know many people who he considered to be sweet. Given their family's history, she should truly hate him, but she'd given him a chance. One he still wasn't sure he'd take.

"Can I ask you a question?" Her voice was tentative, a little nervous.

Instinct made him want to put his guard up, but she'd opened up to him about her mother and he found he wanted to trust her. He withdrew his hand, wrapped it around his glass of vodka. "Of course."

She trailed her finger down the stem of her wine glass. She'd worn a simple black dress tonight with diamond studs in her ears and no other jewelry. Still, she shone as brilliantly as a star everywhere she went. The extra security team tonight had certainly taken notice of her. It was hard not to. But he'd made it clear to Lyosha that she was *his* woman, that everyone should treat her with respect. His longtime friend and head of security had shown a flicker of surprise, but in true Lyosha form had said he'd make sure everyone knew.

"It's none of my business. I'm just curious about you. But if you don't want to answer you don't have to." She rushed out the words, as if she'd been practicing.

"Just ask," he murmured, tension rising inside him. Maybe his brother had been right after all. This would be where she started to ply him for information in an effort to use it against him.

"How is it that you and your brother, ah, half-brother, have the same last name?" She cleared her throat. "I know that your father's last name was..." She trailed off, pain flashing in her expression before she masked it. That was one thing he'd come to learn about her—she didn't hide her emotions as well as she probably thought she did.

Her question wasn't what he'd expected, and easy to answer. He'd been worried she'd want to know more about his past, more about his relationship with his father, or how Viktor had gotten to where he was today. Something she could use against him. But this... She could have found this out from a search.

Even though he knew she could be testing him, that this might be some sort of warm-up question, the tension in his chest eased ever so slightly. "When my father died

I took my mother's name. Ivanov is a very common Russian family name—one of the most common, in fact. Abram's mother had the same last name as well. It's a lucky coincidence." One he was happy for. He liked having that link to Abram. He didn't care that they were technically half-brothers. That shit meant nothing to him. They were true brothers in every sense of the word.

Dominique gave him a knowing smile. "You two are close."

He nodded. "He's a good brother." Even if he did worry too much.

"I...don't know if he likes me very much." She stumbled over the words. "At the hotel the other day, he seemed to know who I was and..." She lifted a shoulder but he could see that it mattered to her.

"Abram is very protective. He thinks...you might be out to hurt me."

She blinked, those gorgeous dark eyes genuinely confused. "Me, hurt you?" Then she laughed, the sweet sound rolling over him like a warm wave.

He realized she thought he meant physically, but he didn't correct her. Viktor half-smiled and lifted a shoulder. "He can be paranoid."

"He's your brother. It's good he worries about you. My cousin, Quinn, is like an older brother to me. Now more than when I was younger."

"Why now?" He'd seen the name Quinn in the file his brother had compiled on her, knew the guy had been a cop and now worked for Red Stone.

"Ah...this might be veering into more heavy stuff than first date conversation."

"This is our second date." There would be a lot more, as far as he was concerned. He reached for her hand again, was glad when she instantly linked her fingers through his. Even her hands were beautiful. She had long, elegant fingers he could easily imagine wrapped around his cock, stroking him until he came.

She laughed lightly and squeezed his hand. "Yeah, you're right. But this is probably oversharing."

"I think we're past that point." His voice was dry.

"True... Okay, fine. After what happened with my mom, Quinn is the first person I called. He, uh, he'd just started working for Red Stone but he'd been a cop before so he swooped in and just took over everything." The adoration on her face was clear. "Even though I was eighteen he refused to let me live on my own. My mom had...cut out that side of the family, her side, because, well, whatever."

"You don't have to tell me any more." The distress that had started to trickle into her expression sliced at him. He didn't want her uncomfortable or in pain. Ever. Which was a stupid thing, considering he couldn't protect her all the time. But he didn't want to be the cause of her distress.

"It's okay, really. I kinda want you to know this about me." She faltered for a moment, but continued. "I moved in with his parents for the first few years I was in college. I, uh, didn't realize it then but I was dealing with depression over everything and they really kept me afloat. They—Quinn and the rest of my family too—were like anchors. I was too caught up in my own bullshit then to be grateful but I know now how lucky I am that they were there for me."

"You are lucky." With the exception of his mother, he'd never had anyone he loved or trusted until Abram. He was glad she'd had family to support her. Her life could have turned out very differently otherwise. He'd seen it happen too.

"This brings me to something I've wanted to tell you." Her cheeks flushed pink, but she trailed off as their server quietly brought their desserts.

Dominique's eyes widened slightly in pure pleasure as the man placed the plate in front of her. Viktor didn't look at his own. He didn't care about the damn food. Hers was a chocolate cup filled with some sort of cream and fresh fruit. There were also fresh strawberries fanned out around it. The entire display was drizzled with chocolate.

"I've always wondered how they make these," she murmured. "The cups are so delicate."

"Balloons," the man said before darting his gaze to Viktor, just a touch of fear in his gaze.

As if Viktor would be angry he'd talked. Jesus, he wasn't that fucking scary. He tried smiling at the man but was pretty sure he failed when the guy flinched. "Balloons?"

The man nodded and looked back at Dominique, his expression quickly morphing to one of appreciation as he talked to her. "The chef dips small balloons into the melted chocolate halfway and they dry in this shape. Once they're done he carefully lets the air out and removes the balloon."

"That's so interesting. I'm going to have to try it," she said.

LOVE THY ENEMY | 143

The man beamed at her before disappearing back to the kitchen.

"You cook?" Viktor asked once they were alone again. He didn't reach for his fork, just watched the expression of pure joy flicker across her features as she took that first bite.

She let out a little moan of appreciation as she nodded. "You want a bite?"

He shook his head, his dick going ridiculously hard. If she took this much pleasure in dessert... He could just imagine what she'd look like when he brought her to orgasm. He'd thought about how he'd do it too, way too many times. He'd never brought a woman to his house but he was obsessed with the idea of her stretched out on his bed, all his for the taking. He wanted to take his time with her, to have her begging for him to fill her.

"You're missing out. And yes, I do like to cook—baking, mostly—though I don't get to as much as I'd like because of work."

His gaze strayed to her mouth as her tongue darted out to swipe cream off her bottom lip. He had to actually bite back a groan at the sight. He'd been with women who knew how to seduce, how to do everything right—because it was all choreographed and fake. With Dominique, he knew there was no artifice.

Even if she was driving him crazy.

He had the irrational urge to shove everything off the table and take her right here. Which was beyond insane. But she made him want to lose control, something he didn't like. He rubbed the back of his neck and glanced around the restaurant.

The extra security was in place and very discreet. After that mugging he didn't care if he was being paranoid. He wanted to make sure Dominique was safe. He just hated that he had no control over what happened to her when she was at home. He couldn't very well insist she keep a security guard with her. Even *he* knew that was insane and would push her away from him.

So he planned to be with her as much as he could. At least then he could protect her. Past that, however, he was in completely new territory. Sex before had always been detached, unemotional. Now...he wanted something different with Dominique. He wanted to make sure she was completely satisfied. Unfortunately he wasn't sure how fast he should move. The more primal part of him said he was moving way too fucking slow. That they should be in bed right now. She should be flat on her back while his face was buried between her legs.

He scrubbed a hand over his face. "You said you wanted to tell me something before?"

She set her fork down even though half of the dessert was still unfinished. "It's not a big deal." But something about her body language said otherwise.

He instantly went on alert, that familiar cynicism building inside him. He hated that he kept expecting something to go wrong, that he was expecting her to stab him in the back.

"It sort of ties in with what I was telling you about my family stuff... I just don't have a lot of experience with dating." Her cheeks flushed that sexy shade again as she watched him.

He felt like she was leaving something out, that he was missing something as she stared at him with those big eyes. "I don't either."

She huffed out a little laugh. "Somehow I think you have more experience than me." This time her cheeks went crimson and he wanted to know exactly what she was thinking.

"I've never had a relationship." The words were out before he could stop himself. If she was running some scam on him and *did* want to hurt him, she'd have already done her homework on him. She'd already know what he was telling her. Still, saying the words out loud made him feel too exposed. He knew he was probably going to regret telling her this, but fuck it. She'd been open with him—even if it was part of some con game she was running. "The first woman I ever thought I loved turned out to be a paid escort. Paid by my father to keep tabs on me."

Dominique let out a horrified gasp, her eyes widening. "What?"

His lips pulled into a thin line as he shoved the anger and shame back down. He'd moved past that part of his life. "He was a bastard through and through. Thought I wanted to take over his organization."

Viktor snorted at the thought. Nothing could have been further from the truth. Back then he'd been working on a way to escape, to get out and start his own legal businesses. He'd wanted nothing to do with his father.

"In my twenties I used to fight in his illegal rings." Partially for the money he'd made betting on himself, and partially so others in his father's organization would never forget that he could easily kill them. He'd always known he'd one day break off on his own and all those men would remember how he'd beaten men bloody. The visceral reminder was better than anything he could ever say. He cleared his throat. "She was at one of them—by chance, I thought."

She'd been so damn sweet—though it had all turned out to be a lie. Everything about her had been a lie.

The humiliation he'd felt when he'd discovered the truth was something he'd never forget. "Since then I've only used escorts. You're the first woman I've ever wanted to take out like this, on a real date." *More than date.* But he left that part out. It didn't matter now anyway. Now that she knew the truth about him she'd get up and walk out of here and never look back. Which was what he knew he deserved. He might be a bastard but he wanted her to know everything about him so she could just leave. He didn't deserve a woman like her. Better to cut this off now before he fell even deeper.

"Oh, Viktor." She reached across the table and slid her fingers through his, holding his hand tight.

Her reaction made him still, even as a tiny spark of...hope flared inside him. She didn't seem disgusted by him and he'd given her an easy out. An easy way to tell him to fuck off and never call her again. "You understand what I'm saying, that I've only ever fucked escorts." His words came out harsh.

She flinched when he said 'fucked' but she nodded. "Yeah, I totally got that. I'm so sorry that your fa-ther...that you got hurt like that."

LOVE THY ENEMY | 147

He pulled his hand back. "I wasn't hurt," he snapped. He'd been stupid and naïve, and it had taught him a valuable lesson. But something told him that if Dominique ever hurt him that same way, he might never recover. She fucking terrified him in so many ways.

The look in her eyes was something a lot like sympathy as she picked up her wine glass. "I'm still sorry."

He started to respond just as a burst of staccato gunfire erupted from just outside the restaurant—in the lobby of the hotel.

CHAPTER TWELVE

Dominique jumped as pops sounded nearby. It took a moment for it to register that it was freaking gunfire! Before she could even think about moving, Viktor had a weapon out and grabbed her around the waist, dragging her to the kitchen.

Panic slammed through her as she ran next to him, her heels making it difficult, but Viktor didn't slow. He had a hold on her and wasn't letting go. She was vaguely aware of other men moving out of the woodwork like shadows, guns in their hands as Viktor barked out orders.

It was complete chaos and she wanted to cover her ears, to block out the shooting. This was nothing like the movies. Her ears rang and her heart pounded wildly in her chest as they breached the swinging kitchen door.

The chef she'd met earlier was standing next to an industrial stove, terror on his face as he remained frozen in place.

Viktor shouted at another man who Dominique had met earlier. Lyosha. If she'd thought Viktor looked scary, this guy was even more so. Tattoos crept up under the top of his shirt, covering part of his neck. He might look like a brainless thug but his sharp green eyes seemed to take in everything. And he didn't appear to like what he saw when he looked at her.

Viktor said something to him in Russian and pushed her to him. She wanted to argue but was almost numb. The man's jaw tightened and it was clear he wanted to argue as well, but he nodded once.

"Stay with him no matter what. He'll keep you safe," Viktor snapped at her before disappearing back out the swinging kitchen door.

She took a step after him, not really to go with him, but to keep him with her. Right now it felt as if her insides would break apart from the adrenaline pumping through her. Her fight or flight response was going haywire and she was having a hard time keeping it together.

A strong hand grasped her upper arm. "Come with me." Lyosha pulled her with him.

"Where's Viktor going? What's happening?" She was terrified for him, that he'd run back into where men were shooting.

He didn't respond, just looked over at the chef and shouted for him and the server to follow. The two men hurried after them as Lyosha tugged her through another door, none too gently—but not before checking outside it. She heard the distant pop of another gunshot, then nothing. Fear for Viktor swelled inside her. What if he'd been hurt?

Her heart continued that erratic beat as they stepped out into a small hallway she realized must be used for employees. "Where's Viktor gone?" She wondered if it was a stupid question but she couldn't believe he'd just raced back out toward the gunfire even if he did have a gun. "Has anyone called the police?"

But the man just hurried down the hallway, his gun at the ready as he stopped four doors down. "We'll be safe in here. There's an extra exit if necessary." He stood back and motioned the three of them into what turned out to be a storage room.

Bins marked with different holiday decorations were stacked on tall metal racks that went all the way up to the ceiling. There was another door on the other side of the small space just as Lyosha had said.

"What's going on?" she asked quietly as he shut the door. Her entire body was trembling so she wrapped her arms around herself. "You can talk now that we're safe," she snapped when he still didn't respond.

He pinned her with a hard look. "I don't know what's going on. Someone is stupid enough to attack Viktor and I should be out there with him. Not watching you three," he muttered, his jaw tightening again.

"Then go if he needs your help!" She hated that Viktor had raced right back into whatever dangerous situation without knowing what he was getting into. The thought of him injured or worse sent another jolt of fear through her. Especially after everything he'd just told her. She couldn't believe his own father had done that to him— well she could, knowing who his father had been, but she still hated it. Viktor had looked as if he hated himself as he admitted to her he'd only been with escorts.

Lyosha simply frowned at her but didn't respond, just pulled his phone out of his pants pocket when it buzzed. After a short conversation in Russian he shoved it back into his pocket then opened the door a fraction.

Hope bloomed inside Dominique that Viktor was there, but another man...Kir was there. The blond-haired, blue-eyed man seemed to have an easy smile for everyone. Now his expression was tight but after murmuring quietly to Lyosha, the other man stepped back and let Kir in.

"Protect the woman with your life." *Or else*, seemed to be the unspoken words that followed. Lyosha's words were sharp, deadly, and sent a frisson of fear down her spine.

Yeah, she was glad he wanted Kir to keep her alive, but the way he spoke was scary. Okay, everything about him was terrifying.

Kir turned to look at all of them as Lyosha left, and half-smiled. "Everything's okay. We'll be in here for just a little bit," he said calmly, his words having a soothing effect on all three of them. "The threat has been neutralized so don't worry. And Viktor's fine," he added before she could ask. "He sent me here to keep an eye on you. To keep you safe."

That was all she needed to hear—that Viktor was okay. Yeah, she had a lot more questions but knowing he was unharmed allowed her to take a deep breath and let some of her panic go. She leaned against one of the racks and turned to look at the other two men who were standing in what looked like a state of shock. Especially the chef. His dark eyes were wide and his entire body was trembling as he more or less stared blankly at her.

She pulled one of the bins off a rack. "Why don't you sit?"

He nodded and did as she said as if he was on autopilot.

"You should probably ask for a raise after tonight," Dominique said to the server, hoping to dispel some of the tension in the small room.

Kir was standing guard and clearly not interested in making the two men feel better, and when she was nervous she tended to talk.

The server let out a shaky laugh but she could see some of the tension leave his shoulders. "No kidding. I'm Eric, by the way."

She forced a smile, glad he seemed to be handling things okay. "I'm Dominique."

* * *

Viktor eyed the fallen bodies, anger a live wire inside him, pulsing and ready to strike out at whoever had ordered this.

He didn't recognize any of the men, and from experience he knew that these guys would be hired muscle. There were six men in all, each one wearing a bulletproof vest and armed to the teeth. They didn't have on more tactical gear, however. Which made Viktor think they weren't that well trained. Careful not to move the body too much, he pulled down the shirt of one and saw what he knew was a prison tattoo.

When he saw Lyosha striding across the lobby strewn with dead bodies, he frowned. "Why are you here?"

"Kir is with the woman and the others. They're fine." His words were almost dismissive, but Viktor knew better. He could see the worry in Lyosha's gaze, faint that it was. "My priority is you. Are we calling the police or not?"

He looked around again. His men were all law-abiding citizens and worked for the security division of his company directly under Lyosha. He was their boss and from experience he knew they'd do whatever he said. "Someone could have heard the gunfire and called it in," he finally said. He absolutely hated involving the police but sometimes it was better to show that he had nothing to hide. And getting rid of half a dozen bodies was doable, but not easy. He'd rather let the police take care of them and have all this on the record.

Lyosha nodded, clearly on the same page. "I'll photograph all the dead men, remove any personal items—if there are any—and take their fingerprints before we call."

"Good. I need you to take Dominique out of here. Kir can make sure the other two get home safely. I'm going to tell the police I was going over the layout of our new plans when we were blindsided. It will be like Dominique and the other two were never here."

Lyosha nodded again. "Good. The chef is about to piss his pants, if he hasn't already. I'll make sure they know they'll be compensated for their silence."

Viktor nodded. It would be easier this way, less messy. He didn't want Dominique dragged into anything and she didn't deserve to get hauled to the police station where she'd be questioned for hours. No, she should be at his home, safe and resting. Her condo was easy to breach so that wasn't an option. He needed her where he could control the environment more. "I'll go talk to Dominique but I want you to take her to my home."

Lyosha's eyebrows raised. "I should be with you."

"I need someone I trust with her. I need to know she's safe while I'm dealing with the cops." And Lyosha had been his driver for years, had joined him after he'd split from his father's organization.

"Fine. But are you sure you can trust her?" There was no malice in the question, the only reason Viktor reined in his temper.

"Why?" Viktor wondered if his brother had said something about their history, but he immediately dismissed that. Abram would never betray his confidence.

Lyosha glanced around at his men and barked out an order for them to start taking fingerprints of the dead guys, before he turned back to Viktor. "I know the type of woman you like." He rubbed the back of his neck, clearly uncomfortable. "No disrespect. I just don't know if you should completely trust someone like her, even if she's yours now."

He blinked, realizing Lyosha had misunderstood him before. "She's not an escort—never was. She works for Red Stone. She is my...she's *mine*."

Now Lyosha cursed, as if that was worse than what he'd originally assumed.

Just to get another rise out of him because it was so rare, Viktor added, "She's Porter Caldwell's assistant."

"You're fucking insane," he muttered. "She works for those Boy Scouts?"

He didn't answer, just tilted his head in the direction of one of the employee doors. He needed to see for himself that she was okay and then convince her she should go with Lyosha. From what he knew of her, he figured Dominique would argue and want to stay, but it wasn't happening. He wanted her gone, mainly because he didn't want the police to tie her to him. He'd been legit for a while but he didn't want to give some asshole cop an excuse to harass the woman he'd fallen for.

Hurrying down the hallway, he texted Kir to let him know they were on their way. As they reached the door to the storage room, Kir peered out, his weapon in hand.

The door quickly shot open and Dominique practically shoved Kir out of the way as she hurried to him. Later he'd have to tell her that she couldn't do that—that in a situation like this she needed to remain behind one of his men at all times until they knew for a fact that everything was clear, but...he liked the worry for him he saw on her face.

Not the actual worry, but he liked that she cared for him enough to be concerned.

"Are you okay?" She grabbed his upper arms, looking him up and down, her body slightly trembling.

"I'm fine." He pulled her into his arms, needing to comfort her, to actually hold her. She was heaven in his arms, soft and sweet and his.

It was a foreign sensation to comfort another person, but he smoothed a hand down her spine and murmured to her in Russian. He knew she wouldn't understand and he truly didn't give a shit that Lyosha and Kir could understand him. If she played him for a fool he'd deal with the fallout. Right now, the only thing he knew was that his woman was upset and he needed to reassure her.

"What happened?" Her voice was muffled, her face buried against his chest.

"Not sure yet." He couldn't give her any details, not now. Getting her out of here was the most important thing.

She pulled back to look at him, just a hint of tears glistening in her dark eyes. "I was so worried about you," she whispered.

He cupped her cheek and brushed his lips over hers. He knew they didn't have time for this, but he just wanted a taste, to reassure her the situation was under control. "Everything's okay," he murmured, pulling back. "I need you to go with Lyosha. He's going to take you to my place. I've got to stay and talk to the cops but I'll tell you anything you want to know when I get there."

She took a step back, her eyebrows drawing together. "I should be here to talk to the police too."

"No." She frowned at his abruptness but he needed her gone. *Now.*

"Viktor—"

"Kir's taken the other two. They're fine leaving." Lyosha's voice made them both turn.

Viktor noticed that Dominique stepped closer to him—away from Lyosha. "See, they're gone too. It'll be easier with you gone as well. No questions from the police, no making a report, nothing. You can go and relax and—"

"And leave you to deal with everything by yourself?" she demanded, turning her full attention to him again. "I'm staying." She crossed her arms over her chest.

"No. You're not." Damn it, he needed her safe. He was used to people following his orders. Always. "If you stay you'll have to lie to the police about the other two not being here. Because they're gone now."

She bit her bottom lip and looked over at the doorway of the storage room. The others had left through the other exit, likely already in a vehicle driven by Kir. "Fine. He can just take me home, then."

"You're going to my place where I know you're safe." That wasn't up for debate. None of this was. He also wanted her where they could pick up where they'd left off. He wanted her in his bed and moaning out his name as he brought her to climax.

She poked at his chest. "Unless you're planning on kidnapping me—"

"I'll do what it takes to keep you safe," he ground out. "I have no idea what tonight was about, who those guys were. So you're going with Lyosha to my place."

Her eyes widened. "What if I say no? You'll seriously just kidnap me?"

He bent down, got right in her face even as he hated the anger—and fear—he saw there. Because it was directed at him. "I will do what it takes to keep you safe," he repeated. "If that means tying you up and hauling you to my home, I'll do it. Don't test me."

She watched him for a long moment, then glanced at Lyosha, who was looking anywhere but at them. Finally she turned back to Viktor and shoved him in the chest. "You're a bastard."

"I know. But I'll be damned if you get hurt because of me." He wanted to comfort her, to kiss her, to do something other than basically kidnap her, but he didn't have time right now for reassuring words. "I'll be there as soon as I can."

After a quick nod at Lyosha, he headed back the way he'd come. Dealing with the cops always made him edgy, but it was something that had to be taken care of.

As soon as it was, he'd go home and face Dominique's wrath. He hated that she was angry at him, but he'd rather deal with that than see her dead from a bullet.

He would keep her safe. Even if she hated him for it. Because after tonight he knew she meant way too much to him already. All he wanted to do right now was take her back to his place and make love to her until they both passed out. To claim her so that she knew who she belonged to.

CHAPTER THIRTEEN

"You should get some rest." Lyosha, who'd brought her back to Viktor's palatial place, had taken off his jacket so that his shoulder holster and guns were showing. He was standing at the window in the living room—*one* of the living rooms—that faced the big driveway.

She'd been worried they should stay away from windows after that attack but he'd assured her that no one would get past the front gate and security.

At first Dominique had been terrified of the guy, and while she was super annoyed with him for forcing her to come here, she'd realized he definitely wasn't going to hurt her. He'd been careful to not even touch her on the way here. And he'd actually been pretty decent, trying to get her to relax. As if that was possible.

"I'm not doing anything until I talk to Viktor," she said. *And rip him a new one.* She couldn't believe him; couldn't believe he'd pretty much kidnapped her and had her sent here by one of his men instead of letting her talk to the police. From everything Lizzy had told her, he wasn't doing anything illegal with his businesses so she couldn't understand his reluctance to let her talk to the police. He'd clearly done nothing wrong—he'd been a victim. Some guys had opened up fire at one his hotels. The whole thing was crazy.

The man made *her* crazy.

"You should listen better," he muttered. A flash of light illuminated him by the window, as if from headlights. The long driveway ended in a huge half-circle in front of the house but there was a four-car garage as well.

Hope bloomed inside her that it was Viktor. It was well after midnight so he should be back anytime. Or she assumed he would be. She snorted at Lyosha's words. "You think I should be a better kidnapping victim?"

He made an annoyed sound in his throat. "You should listen better to Viktor. He's just looking out for you. He needs his woman not to question him."

A burst of surprised laughter escaped. "Oh my God, you did not just say that. Like what, I should be one of his employees and just jump when he says something? Relationships don't work like that. Not since the nineteen fifties." Not that she knew from experience, not really. But she'd at least had a good example from her parents—until everything went pear-shaped. And it wasn't like she and Viktor were even in a relationship. She'd thought they might be heading that way—until tonight. Now she just wanted to smack him.

"No, you're a woman. You need to let him take care of you." Frowning, he pulled out his cell phone. Whatever he read on the screen had the tension in his shoulders completely easing up.

"Oh sweet Lord, so you're a sexist," she muttered. "Just great." She stood, determined to find Viktor. Because she was pretty sure he was back, if Lyosha's body language and the flash of headlights were any indication.

He pinned her with a penetrating stare. "I'm not sexist. I just think—"

"I really, *really* don't care what you think. Where's Viktor?"

He lifted a big shoulder.

"Fine. I'll find him myself." She swiveled and headed out of the room. She'd taken her heels off hours ago but was still in her dress. The hardwood floor of the foyer was cool against her feet. She hadn't gotten a tour of the place but she could pretty much guarantee Viktor wasn't up the stairs to her right.

There was a huge formal dining room across from the living room she'd just been in, and another door on the other side of it. It had to extend to the rest of the house, and since the garage was on the other side—

"Come on." Lyosha fell in step with her. "I'll take you to him."

She hurried after him as he continued to the dining room at a fast clip. "I'm surprised you're taking me."

"It's better than you running all over this place, getting into things that don't concern you." He shot her a dark look as he opened the swinging door connected to the dining room.

She just rolled her eyes and strode past him into what turned out to be a huge, gorgeous kitchen. Everything in it appeared new.

She didn't get a chance to appreciate any of it before Lyosha ushered her through it to a hallway. Then another one, until he knocked on a heavy-looking wood door with intricate carvings on the outside. It was custom and beautiful.

Viktor opened the door a moment later and much to her annoyance her heart skipped a beat at the sight of him. She could see Abram behind him, leaning against a big desk. Viktor's eyes widened at the sight of her, then he glared at Lyosha. He growled something in Russian but thankfully Lyosha answered in English.

"I told her to take one of the guest bedrooms and offered her new clothes. She said no." He looked at her, seemingly for confirmation.

She nodded, even though a small part of her wanted to throw him under the bus. He was just doing his job and she wasn't going to hold it against him. Even if he annoyed her with his sexist bullshit. "We need to talk," she said to Viktor as the door opened even wider.

His brother stepped past her, giving her an unreadable look as he motioned that Lyosha should come with him.

Viktor moved back so she could enter. "I'm sorry you got dragged into this." For a moment he looked as if he would reach for her, but he let his arms drop. His voice was as exhausted as his expression.

Which made her feel bad. She wanted to comfort him, to wrap her arms around him. But not until they hashed some things out. "I'm really not happy with you, but first…were any of your men hurt? Are you okay with the police?"

"None of my guys were injured and yes, I'm fine. They just had a lot of questions and had to deal with the bodies. It was very time-consuming."

"I'm glad you're okay." She smacked his upper arm once. "But I'm not okay with you kidnapping me."

His jaw tightened as he looked down at her. Without her heels on he actually towered over her. Instead of using his height difference against her, he sighed and went to sit on the edge of the desk. "I'm sorry, Dominique."

The way he said her name sent a shiver of awareness through her. She fought against her reaction. She came to stand in front of him, hating how tired he looked. "Why didn't you let me stay?"

"I just... I didn't want you there, not with the cops and the whole parade of people I knew would be there."

"Why not? You're not into anything illegal, right?"

"Not anymore."

She nodded once. "I know that."

His lips curved up, his smile wry. "Your guys down at Red Stone tell you that?"

She lifted a shoulder. "More or less. So what's the deal, for real? You think I can't handle a few questions from the police?"

"I didn't want you to *have* to. I didn't want you on their radar at all." His words were as harsh as his expression. There was no give there. Now he didn't look tired, just angry and frustrated. "I didn't want you linked to all that death, to me."

"That's stupid. I'm a big girl, I've dealt with a lot in my life and—"

"I know!" He shoved up from the desk but she didn't back down. "I just didn't want you to have to deal with anything else. There was nothing you could tell them, no need for you to be there. I just...wanted you safe." He practically growled the last couple words, his big, sexy body vibrating with tension.

"That's not fair."

He blinked. "What isn't?"

She leaned into him, wrapping her arms around him, taking him off guard if the way he jolted at her touch was any indication. "I've worked up a lot of anger at you the last few hours. I'm still not happy and I seriously hope there's not a next time for this kind of thing, but if there is, just include me in whatever happens. You don't need to protect me."

He smoothed a hand down her spine. "I want to."

She liked the way he held her, how secure he made her feel. "Will you tell me what happened tonight? Or who attacked your hotel?"

Sighing, he pulled back and motioned to one of the chairs. She didn't want to move away from him so she tugged him until he sat, then she sat on his lap. He seemed surprised by it but she didn't care. She might be annoyed with him, but she still couldn't seem to get enough of him.

He wrapped his arms around her, holding her tight. She wasn't sure what cologne he used but the subtle, masculine scent wrapped around her as he sighed. Looking into his face now, it was hard to remember that she'd once been afraid of this man, that she'd hated him.

"Men with guns attacked my hotel. There were half a dozen of them and I don't know who they are or who they worked for. But we're looking into it. We...took their fingerprints. I know the police will do their job, but my people are better equipped. And I need to know who did this." His jaw tightened, his rage clear.

Dominique placed a gentle hand on his chest and shifted slightly against him. His grip around her tightened, his eyes darkening a fraction. His erection was evident but she couldn't focus on that now. "Do you have any ideas?"

He paused and she could see the indecision on his face. "Ideas, yes. The attack was bold, which does narrow it down."

"That's good, right?"

He nodded, his expression wary as he watched her. "I'm not letting you leave my place."

She blinked. "What?"

"Until I figure out who was behind the attack, you're staying with me." His grip on her tightened as if he thought she might bolt.

"Will someone at least go to my place to get my clothes?"

He blinked, his grip loosening a fraction. "You're not arguing?"

"Well, I don't like your tendency to tell me what to do."

"I think you like it a little," he murmured, his voice dropping an octave. His gaze dipped to her mouth, his expression going heated.

She felt that look all the way to her core. Heat flooded her as she shifted against him again. "Maybe I like it in the bedroom." She was pretty sure she would anyway. "But not outside it."

"Hmm."

"Look, I don't want to die, and if someone's targeting you—and they obviously didn't care that I'm with you—

then I'll stay here for now. But I'm going to work Monday." She needed to make sure he knew that before they started kissing and she completely lost any sensible thoughts.

His lips pulled into a thin line but he nodded, one hand sliding up her leg, dipping under the hem of her dress as he moved over her upper thigh.

She sucked in a little breath, enjoying the feel of his callused fingers stroking her skin. She wondered how high he would move.

"I called Porter, told him a little of what's going on and that we'll see how Monday goes. But Red Stone is one of the safest places in the city. You should be fine to go to work."

Annoyance surged through her at his 'do what I say' attitude but it was hard to care as his hand crept higher. His touch was so gentle, his fingers just barely skimming her skin, but he still scorched her, sending tingles of awareness straight to all her nerve endings.

He knew he was making her crazy. His blue eyes looked somehow darker in the dim light of his office, the hunger rolling off him palpable as he watched her carefully.

She sucked in a breath when he reached the silky edge of her panties. She was already wet for him, her nipples hard against her bra cups. Anticipation hummed through her as she waited for him to move just a bit, to touch her exactly where she wanted, where she ached for him.

"Stay in my bed tonight?" he asked, his voice hoarse, his gaze focused on her mouth as he teased a finger under the edge of her panties. He was basically touching her hip, nowhere near where she wanted him to be, and yet she had goose bumps all over.

Swallowing hard, she nodded. She definitely wanted that. And she knew what he was asking. Which meant... "I need to tell you something. It's not a big deal, really." Oh God, this was harder than she thought. A small part of her didn't want to say it at all but he needed to know. "I'm...a virgin."

He blinked once, as if he hadn't heard her right. Lightning fast he slid his hand out from under her dress and smoothed it into place. Then he patted her leg as if he didn't know what to do with his hand. He looked a little like a deer caught in headlights as he cleared his throat.

"I still need to do a little work," he said, moving to stand, sliding her off his lap as he did. "But I'll make sure Lyosha gets you settled in a guest room."

His words were like a slap of ice water against her face as what he said registered. He was sending her away to a guest room; basically rescinding the offer of taking her to his bed. Because what, he couldn't handle her being a virgin? Embarrassment flooded her as he strode from the room, practically running away from her. She hadn't thought he'd care. Not so much that he'd flee from her as if she had some disease.

Stupid tears pricked her eyes as she sat on one of the chairs. Part of her wanted to go after him, but she didn't know what to say. It was clear he had no interest in her now. That hurt worse than she could have imagined.

CHAPTER FOURTEEN

Viktor scanned another file of potential suspects, still trying to narrow down who the hell hated him enough to come after him so boldly. This had personal written all over it. Personal and...a little amateurish. The attack hadn't been as well thought out as it could have been and the point of entry was stupid, considering all the other entrances for the hotel.

He clicked to another file but wasn't truly seeing anything, not enough to digest any real information. All he could think about was Dominique and her words to him. It seemed impossible that she was a virgin. He hadn't known what to say, how to respond. She might as well have sucker punched him.

"She's settled in." Lyosha's voice made him look up from his computer. The other man leaned against the doorframe of Viktor's office, his expression annoyed.

Viktor frowned. "What?"

"Why are you still here and not upstairs? Or why isn't she in your fucking bed?"

He gritted his teeth, ignoring the questions. Leaning back in his chair, exhaustion crept in on him. "I need to read over these files."

"You already know what's in them."

It was true. "Why do you care what I'm doing?"

Lyosha lifted a shoulder. "Just wondering what you did to make your woman cry."

Viktor was standing before he realized he'd moved. Guilt punched through him. "She was crying?"

"No. But it's good to know you care if she does. And for the record, she looked like she wanted to. What the fuck are you doing down here?"

There weren't many people who talked to him so freely but Lyosha had been his friend for many years. Didn't mean Viktor wanted to have this conversation. Not with him, not anyone. "You didn't even trust her a few hours ago," he muttered, sitting back down. He should just go to bed, but he didn't want to go alone—because he knew he wouldn't sleep. He'd be too busy fantasizing about Dominique. And as soon as he had a thought, just as quickly he'd feel like a fucking perv. She didn't deserve someone like him for her first time, someone whose hands were stained with blood. Still...the thought of being her first, introducing her to sex... *Damn it.* He scrubbed a hand over his face. He was too damn conflicted.

"Don't tell her, but I like her. It's clear she cares about you." Lyosha's mouth curved up in his version of a smile. "I had fun messing with her earlier about her role as 'your woman.' For a moment I thought she might hit me."

Viktor could imagine what his friend had said. "You're an asshole."

"I know. Now what's the problem?"

Yeah, not having that conversation. "Shut the door."

Lyosha immediately went into work mode, stepping inside and shutting it quickly behind him. "What's up?"

"I looked over your report and agree with the top three suspects, but...I think they might be getting information from someone who works for me and Abram." He couldn't be sure, but he didn't like how Dominique had been mugged while out with him. Then that bold attack with her there at the hotel. Not many people had known about his plans last night—and even fewer the night of the mugging. The three people he suspected he'd done business with before and things had gone south when Viktor had bought them out—legally. He hadn't actually screwed any of them. They'd been paid fairly, but some people couldn't take what they perceived as losing.

The other man nodded. "I've already started running security checks on anyone who has direct access to you or Abram. Digging into financials and phone records to start. If I learn nothing from either of those, I'll move on to another step but I think I'll have something by tomorrow morning." He glanced at his watch. "Later this morning."

"What about the fingerprints or facial IDs?" One way or another they were going to figure out who'd come after him. Getting that information from the dead, would-be hit men was a good place to start. If the dead men had been paid already he'd just follow the money trail back to the payer.

"Still working on it. Those programs take time to run all possible matches. I've got an alert set up on my phone and yours. You'll get a notice when something pops up."

"Good. Go get some sleep." Normally he didn't have so much security at his house, just a basic two-man team. But for now he was keeping everything locked down tight. Even Abram was here and had brought Lucy just in case she was targeted.

Lyosha snorted as he pulled open the door. "You too."

Once Viktor was alone he shut his computer down and tried to convince himself to go to his own bedroom. Alone.

His room was attached to his office so he *should* just step right next door. Instead he found himself heading for the guest room Dominique was in.

He'd been an asshole before but he hadn't been able to handle what she'd told him, hadn't even known what to say. Hell, he still wasn't sure he could deal with it.

What did he know about virgins?

His hands were dirty in more ways than one. He broke out into a sweat just thinking about touching her now. Even though he desperately wanted to, Dominique deserved better than him.

Even when he'd told her about his sexual past she hadn't judged him, she'd just looked as if she wanted to give him a fucking hug. Which was almost worse. He'd told her to give her a way to walk out on him. But she hadn't taken it.

Then he'd walked out on her like an asshole when she'd been honest with him. Made herself vulnerable with him.

She didn't deserve that.

When he reached the door of the bedroom he knew she was in he had to wipe a damp palm on his pants. He immediately cursed himself for the weakness. The woman had turned him into someone he didn't recognize but it was hard to give a shit when she opened the door wearing a T-shirt that was most definitely his. Lyosha must have given it to her. It barely came to mid-thigh. He wanted to drop to his knees, shove that shirt up and press his face to her belly, beg her forgiveness, then make her melt and settle his mouth over her pussy. He wouldn't stop until she'd gone over the edge and was crying out his name.

Her mouth tight, she crossed her arms over her chest—and given the outline of her full breasts, it was clear she wasn't wearing a bra. "Is everything okay?"

He shook his head and pushed into the room past her. The bed was slightly rumpled and only a single lamp was on, casting the room into shadows. "No."

She gasped, dropping her arms. "What are you doing?"

He shut the door behind him and forced his gaze to her face—even though the sight of her long, bare legs called to his most primal side. He wanted them draped over his back, her feet digging into him as he made her come against his mouth. Even though the sane part of him told him to walk away, to just apologize and leave, he didn't think he could. Not when he was standing here, looking into her beautiful face and knowing he'd never meet another woman like her.

"I came to apologize. I acted like an asshole."

She nodded. "Yeah, you did."

"I'm sorry. I...it wasn't about you. When you said you were a virgin I worried about hurting you." More like tainting her with who he was.

To his surprise, she rolled her eyes and went to sit on the edge of the bed. "People have sex every day. I'm not some petite doll you have to worry about hurting. Something you already know. So I accept your apology but I don't buy that crap about not wanting to hurt me. You made me feel really bad about myself." She wrapped her arms around her middle again, the simple action putting a wall up between them.

He'd done that and he hated it. He didn't want there to be anything between them.

He scrubbed a hand over his face. "I know," he rasped out. "I'm truly sorry. I'm in new territory here and you scare the shit out of me." The admission cost him but she was worth it.

Her eyebrows drew together. "*I* scare you?" Her voice was incredulous.

Nodding, he went to sit on the edge of the bed. Her sweet scent was subtle, but the exotic, floral notes teased him. "I've never been with a woman like you. I've never known a woman as sweet as you. I keep giving you reasons to walk away and you keep surprising me. I've...fallen for you pretty hard." Laying himself completely bare was almost too much.

Her dark eyes softened just a fraction. Taking it as a good sign, he scooted a few inches closer. The need to touch her was overwhelming, but he resisted.

"You deserve someone better than me for your first time." Though if they *had* a first time, he was going to try damn hard to make sure it was the best she ever had. No. He wanted to make sure he was her *only* lover from this point forward. Strangely, the thought of being in a committed relationship didn't scare him as much as he expected. What did scare him was if she didn't want the same thing.

"Why would you say that? Yeah, you're a little rough around the edges sometimes—and annoyingly bossy—but you're a good man." She closed the distance between them until their knees were touching. "You hurt me earlier but I still haven't changed my mind about us, about..." She trailed off, gesturing between them, but she didn't need to finish.

His gaze strayed to her mouth. Just the thought of brushing his lips over hers, of pinning her beneath him as he brought her to orgasm, was making it hard to think. To breathe.

He wasn't a good man. The words stuck in his throat. He wanted to tell her the things he'd done, that he'd killed his own father. Killed others. Always to protect himself, but he still had blood on his hands. He couldn't force the words out though. Not when she was looking at him with those big, dark eyes and all he wanted to do was kiss her, to make her his.

He cleared his throat. "I haven't been with anyone in over a year." He'd gotten tired of paying for sex, of feeling no connection. "And I've been tested. I'm clean—and I have all the paperwork. You can see it whenever you want." He mentally crossed his fingers that she still wanted him at all. It had sounded like she did, but he didn't want to make an assumption.

When she pushed up from the bed, his hopes withered into nothing. She was going to tell him to leave. He prepared for the blow, for her to tell him that it wasn't happening.

Until she stripped the T-shirt over her head, revealing the body he'd been fantasizing about since the first night he'd seen her.

His cock shoved at his pants as she dropped the shirt to the ground. He devoured her with his eyes, afraid to touch her.

Her breathing was erratic and the pulse point in her neck was going crazy. Long, blonde hair cascaded around full breasts he wanted to cup, kiss, stroke. They rose and fell, her pink nipples already hard. Her slender waist flared into full hips and her pussy was covered by a thin scrap of black, lacy material she would soon be losing.

He swallowed hard, met her gaze as he stood. A good man would probably tell her they didn't need to do anything tonight. She'd been through a hell of a lot in the past few hours and despite what she'd said, he knew he didn't deserve her.

But it was already too late for that. There was no way he was walking away from her.

He cupped her cheek and realized his hand was trembling. If anyone could fuck him up, it was her. He'd looked down the barrel of a gun before with a certainty he was going to die and hadn't felt a sliver of the fear he did now.

Well, more than the fear that he'd screw things up— or that she'd eventually walk out on him when she realized she could do better.

Even with all that jumbled in his head, he'd never been so turned on in his life.

He'd never had slow or sweet sex, wasn't even sure he could. Even with his ex, the one person he'd thought had loved him, it had been rough and hard. He didn't want that with Dominique.

"Tell me if you don't like something and we'll stop. Promise me." He growled the words, needing to hear her say yes before he completely lost himself in her.

She just gave him a sensual smile and pressed her body to his, standing up on tiptoe to kiss him.

He let go of everything in that moment. He trusted that she'd tell him if they went too far. He covered her mouth with his, cupping her cheek with one hand and gripping her hip in the other. The thin strap of her panties was the only thing between his hand and completely bare skin.

That was going to change now.

Moving quickly, he grasped her ass and lifted her onto the bed. She stretched out on her back, her stomach muscles pulled tight as he crawled over her, caging her in. He was ready to devour every inch of her.

He might not know anything about being with a virgin, but he knew she'd need to be ready for him. Which meant his clothes were staying on until she'd come. He wanted to pleasure her first, to bring her to climax with his mouth before he even got undressed. He'd prove to her that this was about more than just fucking.

"I don't know where to start," he murmured, meeting her gaze. "I want to kiss all of you at the same time."

It must have been the right thing to say because she half-smiled and pushed out a breath as she stroked her hands over his chest. Which was unfortunately still covered.

He wanted to feel her skin to skin but that would happen soon enough. Reaching between their bodies, he barely cupped her covered mound. "Would you like it if I kissed you here?"

Her dark eyes dilated and her cheeks flushed as she made a moaning sound that could have been a yes. That was good enough for him.

Though he wanted to simply bury himself inside her, he forced himself to go slow, to savor this—for both of them. He wanted to work her up to sex, to make sure tonight was all about her.

He was so used to taking charge in the bedroom, to getting exactly what he wanted, that this was virgin territory for him too. With Dominique, she was in control of him even if she didn't know it.

He covered her mouth again, kissed her until she was arching underneath him, her body plastered to his. He'd never had this before, this slow sweetness of just kissing. He loved the almost shy way her tongue flicked against his even as her fingers dug into his back with force, telling him she wanted him exactly where he was. On top of her.

She was soft and slender beneath him, the complete opposite of him and he loved it.

Driven with the need to stroke his tongue against her pussy, he somehow tore his mouth from hers, feathering kisses along her jaw and down the long, elegant column of her neck. Everything about her was elegant, right down to her slender fingers.

She slid them against his scalp, through his closely cropped hair as he moved lower, lower, lower... She moaned as he sucked on a taut nipple.

He lifted his head, watching her reaction. Everything about her was real, right down to her sensual moans. He loved that none of this was scripted, that she was truly enjoying herself. He sucked just a little harder, wanting to see what her reaction would be. He wasn't sure how much experience she had at all so he needed this to be memorable for her.

"Viktor..." Her fingers tightened as she arched her back, trying to shove herself deeper in his mouth.

He groaned against her soft skin, gently palmed her other full breast. She was like the sweetest offering, a dessert he wanted to savor all night. His first time had been with an escort even if he hadn't known it. This was nothing like that. This was...heaven.

His cock was heavy between his legs, aching to fill her body.

But he couldn't screw this up. He needed her wet and begging for him, so turned on that the bite of pain when he entered her wouldn't matter. He had no clue how much it would hurt—he just had to make this good for her and hope it minimized her discomfort later.

Taking him by surprise, she shoved at his head. "You're killing me," she rasped out. Her body writhed under his in the most sensual way, her legs clenching around his waist, her grip tight.

She was basically rubbing herself against him, looking for a release—one he was going to give her with his mouth, fingers, cock.

He moved down to her belly, layered more kisses along the flat plane of her stomach as she lifted her hips, silently begging him for more.

She might be a virgin but she seemed to know exactly what she wanted. He wondered if she'd ever had someone go down on her, but didn't want to ask for a multitude of reasons. This time was just about them.

Crouched between her legs, he kept his gaze pinned to hers as he hooked his finger in her panties and began dragging them down her smooth, tanned legs. She had fine, pale blonde hair on her mound. "Tell me what you want," he demanded. "Say the words." Because he needed to hear them. Some primal part of him wanted her to spell it out.

Her cheeks were flushed, her eyes heavy-lidded. "Kiss me."

"Where?" He wasn't sure why he was pushing, but he wanted to hear the word on her lips. He'd push her more, later, once she was ready. For now, he just wanted to hear—

"My pussy." She whispered the words, as if someone might overhear.

He jerked at hearing the words roll off her tongue, wanted to capture her mouth again and plunge right into her, but first...

He inhaled her sweet scent as he ran a finger down her slick folds. She was soaked, and the knowledge did something primal to him. She made him feel like a fucking caveman with the need to claim her, to make sure everyone knew that this sensual woman was his.

Leaning down, he flicked his tongue over the tiny bud already swollen and peeking out from her folds.

She jerked against him, a shudder racking her.

"So sensitive," he murmured before teasing her with his tongue again, this time with more pressure.

Her hips rolled against his face as he continued kissing and licking her clit. The moaning sounds she made were the most erotic thing he'd ever heard. She wasn't acting. This wasn't a show for him. This was her completely enjoying herself. Her fingers dug into his head and he savored the nip of pain.

When he finally slid a finger inside her, he shuddered at her slickness. She was so damn reactive and this was all for him. He knew he shouldn't care that she'd never been with anyone, and if she had, he wouldn't have given a shit. But to know he was going to be her first made him crazy.

Made him feel honored in a way he was certain he didn't deserve.

But he could be the right man for her. That he knew with a bone-deep certainty. He could give her everything she wanted, take care of her, keep her safe. He knew that no one was entirely safe but he'd make damn sure she had the best of everything.

As he slid another finger into her, she groaned. "Viktor, more. Please." The sweet way she begged made him crazy.

He decided to stop teasing. She was so wet she'd be able to take him fully. But he needed her to come first. She had to have pleasure before that pain. He wouldn't allow anything else.

Increasing the pressure of his tongue, he circled her pulsing clit, relished the way she writhed against his face, her cries growing louder as he teased her. He moved his fingers in and out of her, her tight sheath clenching around his fingers quicker and quicker.

She was close.

He needed her to come. Needed it so bad he was practically shaking.

"Oh... Oh, Viktor..." Her back arched and she dropped her hands from his head, clenching those fingers—the ones he'd imagined wrapped around his cock too many times—into the covers.

He tweaked her clit with just a little more pressure. She was so close. Her inner walls tightened around him faster and faster and he knew the exact moment before she was about to fall over the edge.

Her entire body tightened right before she cried out and let go. His fingers grew even slicker as she found her release. He savored the little ripples of her tight pussy as she reached orgasm.

Lifting his head, he watched her ride through it. Her eyes were closed, her cheeks and chest flushed pink as she continued coming. Eventually she stilled against the covers, her breathing erratic as she opened her eyes to look at him.

Her lips curved up in a sensual smile of pure bliss, looking thoroughly satisfied. "That was amazing," she murmured, instantly reaching for him.

The way she moved for him, her arms outstretched, made his heart swell until he felt it would explode.

He stripped off his shirt and pants, getting undressed in record time. He grabbed a condom from his pocket but she frowned at it and sat up as he crawled back into the bed.

He was rock hard, his cock jutting out so thick and heavy that for the first time in his life he wished he was a little smaller.

She took the condom from him and tossed it away as she grasped his hard length. "I'm on the pill and I don't want a barrier between us the first time."

He couldn't believe she was putting that much faith in him. The fact that she was made him realize that this was a woman he could trust, a woman he was never letting go.

He looked down between their bodies. Watched, mesmerized, as she stroked him oh-so-slowly. Way too gentle for what he normally preferred, but just having her hand on him, he was pretty sure he could come right there if she continued.

He didn't respond about the condom. If she didn't want one, he trusted her to be on the pill. The truth was, he wanted to be inside her bare too. Even the thought was almost too much for the last shred of his control.

Crushing his mouth to hers, he covered her body with his. He grasped her wrist, pulled her hand away from his cock because no way was he coming in her hand. Not this first time.

He'd never wanted a woman like this. Ever. He felt fucking possessed as he positioned himself at her entrance and slowly slid inside her inch by inch. He pulled back just a little so he could see her face, could make sure he wasn't

186 | KATIE REUS

hurting her. Her dark eyes were dilated as he moved into her, her breathing erratic and the pleasure in her gaze crystal clear. She was slick and so tight it took all his control to do this right.

Which was hard when his balls were pulled up tight and all he wanted to do was empty himself inside her. Especially after she'd said she wanted him inside her with no barrier.

Yeah, this woman was his. In a way he hadn't fully comprehended until now. He knew that having her in his life would give him a weakness he'd never had before.

But letting her go wasn't an option. He couldn't live in a world with her and not have her in his life. *Nope. Not happening.*

"You're mine," he growled against her swollen lips. The words came out guttural as he held back the urge to slam into her.

She sucked in a breath, her eyes glazed over with passion as he gave the final push inside her. There was a slight resistance that gave way before he was buried fully inside her.

Her inner walls tightened around him but he didn't move, just watched her carefully, heart pounding. "Is this okay?"

Her lips curved up ever so slightly, her breathing uneven as she nodded. "It's different. I feel very full but...no pain. Promise," she whispered.

The truth in her eyes was clear so he pulled back slowly, gritting his teeth at how good she felt, how tight.

Everything about this moment was so intimate. He wanted to look away, felt too vulnerable as she stared up at him, but he couldn't. This was more than sex to him. More than he could put into words.

He wasn't sure he wanted to. Being with her like this had ripped him in two so that he felt like a different person. A better person with her.

She stroked her fingers down his back as he thrust in and out of her. The sensation of being inside her was too much and not enough. He didn't think he'd ever get enough of her.

She was an addiction he was more than glad to succumb to.

He wasn't sure if she'd be able to have a second orgasm, but he was damn sure going to try. Slowing down his thrusts, he reached between their bodies and tweaked her clit, rubbing with enough pressure he knew she'd like it.

She jerked against him, sucking in a sharp breath as her inner walls started rippling around him. He felt her climax start to build almost immediately, could hear it in the way her breathing grew erratic and out of control.

When she reached down and grabbed his ass, digging her fingers into him in a purely possessive way as she cried out his name, he let go. There was nothing else to do.

Her name was on his lips as they both came. He thrust into her long and hard as he found his release. It felt as if he climaxed forever. He buried his face against her neck, breathing her in as his orgasm finally subsided.

She wrapped her arms around him tight, holding him so close he never wanted to let her go. Her embrace made him feel honored and possessive at the same time. "That was wonderful," she murmured, her voice just a little sleepy.

He couldn't find his voice so he just held her, trying to come to terms with how his life had just shifted.

And he was done worrying that she was going to stab him in the back, that she was working some angle against him. This, what she'd given him... He simply knew now that she wasn't waiting to hurt him.

The only way she could hurt him was by walking away.

CHAPTER FIFTEEN

"I could lie here all day," Dominique murmured against Viktor's solid chest. She wasn't sure what time it was but it was early. At least it was Saturday so she didn't have to worry about work.

His hand stroked up and down her back in a lazy rhythm. Though he was hard, he hadn't made a move to touch her since their last bout of lovemaking. Which was good because she was too sore. She traced her finger over the curves of one of his many tattoos. When he'd completely bared himself to her she'd been surprised by how many he truly had. Not to mention the multitude of long faded scars that covered his body—mainly his torso and arms. One day she would ask him what the tattoos meant and how he'd gotten the scars.

After their first time he'd been so sweet, surprising her by getting a warm cloth and cleaning between her legs. It had been so intimate, so...unexpected. She'd quickly learned that he did a lot of unexpected things. He'd made her so angry last night, just taking over and ordering her back to his house, but she could see that it was from a place of protectiveness. And it certainly didn't make her like him any less. If anything, his bossiness turned her on. Not that she was going to tell him that. Not yet anyway. He'd probably turn into a super caveman if she did.

"I would like that very much. How are you feeling?" He reached between her legs, cupping her sex in a purely possessive move. His big hand was gentle though.

Feeling her cheeks heat up, she shifted her head so she could look at him. "A little sore, but good."

His blue eyes heated with hunger but he withdrew his hand and wrapped his arm around her, just holding her close. "I thought you would be."

They'd had sex again a couple hours after that first time. He'd slowly taken her from behind as she gripped the headboard, teasing her clit as he moved inside her. Even thinking about it made a shudder rack through her entire body.

She set her head back on his chest, feeling more content than she had in a long time. "Why do you hire so many Russians? I mean, I know you are Russian. I just wondered if there was a reason," she said after a few minutes. There was so much about him she wanted to know.

"That's a long answer." The rumble of his chest under her head vibrated through her.

She smiled against his hard body, wishing she wasn't so sore right now. "I don't have anywhere to be."

He didn't respond for so long, she thought he wouldn't at all. "I had already started to break away from my father before he...died. He was a violent, vindictive asshole so I had to move slowly, setting up various accounts and a lot of stuff I won't bore you with. For lack of a better term, he was a gangster. He'd created his own little empire right here in Miami but not all the men who worked for him did so willingly. From the time I was a kid I watched him carefully—watched his people carefully. I knew who would break away from him when I made my move."

"He died before that though, didn't he?" Viktor had told her that his father had left him her family's house as part of his trust and she couldn't believe that he would have done that if Viktor had cut ties.

She felt Viktor move slightly, as if he was nodding. "Yeah. There was another man who'd always been in competition with me." He paused again, and she guessed he was choosing his words carefully. "He wanted my father's empire, wanted me out of the way. I wanted the same thing essentially so I made a deal with him. I took the men I knew who were loyal to me and we severed ties from that life in a clean break. I'd already started working legitimate side businesses, so the transition wasn't difficult. As long as I didn't try to take any of his criminal enterprises we had no problem."

She looked up at him. The room was dim except for a few streams of light coming in through one of the curtain-covered windows. "He just let you go?" She didn't know much about the criminal lifestyle but that sounded too easy.

Viktor gave her a dark smile. "He had no choice. Not unless he wanted a war."

She bit her bottom lip. "Is there a possibility he's the one who attacked you last night?"

He snorted, his expression easing. "No. He's actually at the bottom of my list. We haven't had contact in years. I stay out of his way and he stays out of mine. The people who attacked last night weren't pros."

"You still keep pretty intense security at your house." She knew that even the Caldwell brothers didn't have the kind of security he did. Not actual armed guards anyway.

"I never let myself get complacent. I can't afford to." He cupped her cheek, his touch gentle. "I'll never risk your safety either. Don't doubt that."

"I don't." She might not have known him that long, but she didn't doubt him. He made her feel...happy in a way she hadn't been in a long time. Which was hard to swallow. She turned her face away from his hold and lay back on his chest.

He stiffened slightly. "What?"

"Nothing... Okay, I feel a little guilty being so happy with you. It makes me think of my mother and then I get so angry at *her*." Shame swelled inside her for feeling angry at all. "She left me. I feel like...she didn't love me enough. Like I wasn't worth sticking around for. Which is stupid, I know." Her throat grew tight as the mix of long-buried emotions shattered inside her. She hated feeling like that.

His hold tightened ever so slightly. "My father was an evil man who ground people into the dirt. The fact that she endured being with him... She loved you very much, Dominique. That's something you should never doubt."

His words soothed all the jagged edges. She didn't respond, just let him hold her. She wasn't sure how long they stayed there but when her stomach rumbled loudly she buried her face against his chest.

He laughed, the sound so sweet to her ears because he rarely seemed to do it. "I think it's time I got you fed." He reached a hand down, palmed her ass before squeezing possessively. "Then I plan to eat you. Slowly."

His words set her on fire, but if she was going to have enough energy to keep up with him, she knew she should eat something. Then...she hoped they headed right back to the bedroom.

Last night had been amazing. She hadn't expected her first time to be so good. Now she was so glad she'd waited. Being with a man like Viktor who'd been so giving, clearly putting her pleasure before his own, had been incredible. She was pretty sure she'd fallen for him. It didn't seem to matter that her head said this was way too fast. Her heart wasn't listening.

* * *

He couldn't concentrate on anything today. Not after last night's failure. He'd hired those men specifically because of their shock tactics and penchant for violence. They were supposed to have killed Viktor's men and taken the woman.

Time was running out and he still needed her as a bargaining chip. He'd eventually kill her, but not until he got what he wanted. Then he'd kill her and Viktor. His brother too, because there was no way Abram would let his brother's death go unpunished.

It was Ivanov's own fault, for coming after him first. The stupid Russian liked to hide behind a mask of civility, claiming that the things he did weren't personal, just business. Well it was fucking personal to him.

With a trembling hand he dialed his contact.

The man answered on the fourth ring, his voice tight. "What?"

"What's the security situation like?"

"Tight. Everyone is locked down and..." A door shut, then, "Both women are locked down as well. Both here."

Here meant Viktor's house. "I want the woman." He didn't need to specify which one. The assistant would have been a decent choice, but knowing that Viktor truly cared for Dominique Castle, that she wasn't some whore he was paying, made her the *only* choice.

"Too bad for you."

He gritted his teeth, forced his voice to remain even. "Two hundred fifty grand in your account if you get her to me by this afternoon."

The man sucked in a breath. "That's still not enough for my life. Because he will hunt me to the end of the earth if I take her."

"He won't be around that long. Once I get her I'll be able to bargain with him for what I want. Then I'll pay you five hundred grand, with the promise that I'll kill him *and* his brother. Once that's done you'll be able to start over somewhere with a nice chunk of money."

Seconds ticked by. One, two, three... "I'll do it. I want that boat of yours too. The one in the marina."

Greedy bastard. Maybe he'd kill him too. He would tidy up all loose ends. "Agreed. Bring her to my office. Call me on your way. I'll meet you in the loading area."

"As soon as I get my money, consider it done."

Pleased with himself, he ended the call. He'd pay him the first deposit, but he'd never pay the five hundred grand. No, he'd kill his contact first.

Soon he'd have that bitch and Viktor would be at his mercy. Opening his desk drawer he pulled out a little packet of cocaine, dipped his finger into it and spread it across his gums. Then he took one hit.

Just one to keep him focused. He wasn't an addict. He just liked the way it made him feel, that rush of adrenaline that helped him to keep working longer hours.

Nothing was going to go wrong. Not like last night. With the exception of that snafu, everything else was falling into place.

Once he got Viktor where he wanted him, he was going to kill the bastard himself. He'd make sure Viktor begged him for death by the time he was through with him.

CHAPTER SIXTEEN

Dominique opened the refrigerator in Viktor's kitchen and stared at the neatly stacked containers of food, and bright fruit and vegetables stocked in the crispers. He hadn't been kidding when he said anything she wanted would be in here. He'd apparently prepared for the zombie apocalypse. Which was fine with her.

She might hate that there was a threat hanging over their heads, but she wasn't going to complain about getting to spend time at Viktor's place. The man had completely stolen her heart and she simply liked being with him. Right now he was in his office with his brother and Lyosha, going over...something. She wished they were back in bed together. Sex was definitely as good as her friends had made it out to be and she was having fun exploring it with him.

"I was hoping I'd find you." A female voice made her turn away from the fridge. Which was just as well—she wasn't sure what she wanted anyway.

She turned to find the petite assistant she'd sort of met the other day. "Hi...Lucy, right?" Viktor had mentioned something about her being here too.

The woman smiled as she leaned against the center island. A book, towel and bottle of sunscreen were in her hand and she was wearing a sheer cover-up that didn't do much to hide her bikini. "Yeah. I'm stuck here too until further notice. You okay after last night? I know that you were at the hotel."

Dominique nodded, glad she didn't have to lie. It was clear both brothers must trust Lucy if she knew Dominique had been at the hotel when even the police didn't. "Yeah, I'm good. A little freaked out but Viktor's place is great if we have to stay on lockdown." Only because the man himself was under the same roof.

"Right? Listen, while they're doing whatever they're doing, I'm taking a break for once and soaking up some sun by that monstrosity of a pool. Want to join me?"

Since Viktor had a fortified wall surrounding his property and extra security, Dominique guessed that was the only reason it would be okay for them to be by the pool right now. Otherwise he'd probably go into super caveman mode and not let them outside. "Yeah, I'd love to. I need to find out if Viktor has anything I can wear." Or if the guys he'd sent over to her place were back yet with her clothes. Right now she was wearing gym pants Lyosha had found that were about four inches too long and an oversized T-shirt. She felt a little ridiculous even if she was comfortable. "I'll meet you out there?"

Lucy nodded, her smile genuine. "Great. I'll see you in a little bit."

Dominique didn't want to bother Viktor but she didn't think he'd mind. And she really wanted to get to know Lucy since she'd be staying here too. Not to mention Lucy obviously knew the brothers well and Dominique wasn't above asking questions about Viktor. She wanted to know everything about him.

When she reached the hallway that led to Viktor's office she smiled when she saw his driver, Kir, headed her way. He'd been one of the only security people who was actually friendly to her. Mostly Viktor's guys seemed to walk around with perma-frowns.

"Hey, is Viktor—" Her words died when she saw the gun in his hand. It had a silencer on it and was pointed directly at her.

Everything around her funneled out as she stared down the barrel of the weapon. Before she could think about moving, he was next to her, grabbing her elbow in an unforgiving grip.

"You're coming with me," he said quietly, almost a whisper, his voice hard. "You scream and I'll shoot you in the stomach. It's a bad way to die." He said it as if it was something he knew to be certain.

On instinct she yanked against his hold but he shoved her up against the wall, one hand wrapped around her throat as he pressed the muzzle of the gun to her temple.

"I'll smoke you right here. Nod if you believe me." His eyes were cold, nothing like the friendly man from the last couple days.

She nodded, her throat tight with fear. What if Lucy came back inside and this maniac decided to shoot her?

"You're going to come with me on a short drive. If you're a good girl, you won't get hurt. But if you fight me, I'll just kill you and cut my losses. You gonna fight me?" He leaned closer, his breath hot against her face.

Ice slithered through her veins, making her feel numb and sluggish. Her heart was a drumbeat in her ears as she shook her head. She wouldn't fight him. At least not this very instant. It would be suicide to go up against a man like this. She might not know much about him but he had a gun he wasn't afraid to use and he was most definitely a lot stronger than her.

"Good. Keep your mouth shut and do what I say." He yanked her away from the wall and dragged her down the rest of the hallway.

Her bare feet were silent against the wooden floor, as were his shoes. All she wanted to do was scream for help, to scream the entire house down. But she'd seen the truth in his eyes—Kir would have no problem ending her life. He wouldn't lose a second of sleep over her death. And what if he shot at Viktor...or Lucy? What if an unarmed person came running to her aid and got caught in the crossfire? She couldn't have that on her conscience.

Looking over his shoulder only once, he paused at the door at the end of the hallway. His grip still tight on her arm he opened the door into a large garage. A car, an SUV, a motorcycle and a vintage truck were parked side by side.

Fear hollowed out her chest, making it hard to breathe as he dragged her inside the garage, shutting the door behind them with a resounding click.

"You are going to be the perfect bargaining chip," he muttered more to himself than her.

Instinct told her to fight him, to try to run. She'd always been taught never to get into a vehicle with someone who meant to do her harm. But if she didn't go, she'd be dead for certain. There was nowhere she could run now, no way to overpower him. She'd just have to go along with him and pray there was an opening for escape.

He palmed a set of keys and pressed the key fob. The SUV lights flashed once, a quiet beep indicating it had unlocked.

"You're driving," he ordered, training his gun on her as he hurried her to the driver's seat. "You try anything stupid, I'll shoot your knee first. Now get in." He yanked the door open for her, his weapon trained on her the entire time.

She practically collapsed on the front seat, her legs weak as he slid into the passenger side. He opened the garage with the little remote hooked to the visor.

"Start the vehicle and slowly steer out," he ordered. She risked a glance at him as the door opened. His gun was still in his hand and pointed at her.

Just freaking great.

She swallowed hard and did as he said. The sun was blinding when she first pulled out of the garage

"Fuck," he growled.

She hit the brakes and froze, unsure what she'd done. Then she saw a man wearing dark pants, a casual polo shirt and a shoulder holster with two guns walking toward them.

"No one was supposed to be here during the shift change," Kir muttered. "Don't say a fucking word." Her window started to roll down, Kir controlling it from the middle console as the man approached the driver's side. She realized Kir meant to talk to him.

He couldn't actually think this guy would believe she was leaving dressed like this. Or that Viktor would let her go? No, Kir meant to shoot him. He raised his weapon and on instinct she floored it, the tires squealing as they shot down the driveway.

"Bitch!" He slammed his fist against the dash but surprisingly didn't strike or shoot her. She'd been waiting for the blow. "Don't slow down," he ordered as they zoomed toward the gate. A man stepped out, weapon drawn, but he aimed at the tires.

Pop. Pop. Pop.

The vehicle swerved as the tire blew but she kept her grip on the wheel. The SUV jerked again wildly as she floored it. God, she hadn't even strapped in.

She wanted to scream at the man to move but he kept shooting at the tires.

Kir cursed and jumped into the backseat. She heard the back window rolling down then the muted sounds of gunfire. The man in front of her dove out of the way, behind the huge brick wall that ran the length of Viktor's property.

He wouldn't shoot at Kir because he wouldn't want to hurt her, she realized. It was why he'd aimed for the tires. For a moment she contemplated jumping from the vehicle but at this speed she didn't know if she'd survive.

"When we exit, take a right," Kir ordered, sliding back into the front seat.

She started to put her seatbelt on but he knocked it out of her hand, his expression dark as he sat back and strapped himself in. "Yours stays off. If you try to crash, you're killing yourself."

She gritted her teeth, her adrenaline pumping as she did what he said and took a sharp right. The shot tire was deflating fast, the vehicle getting hard to control as they careened down the street. She didn't have a death wish and right now it was either death from car crash or a bullet to the stomach. She didn't like either of those options.

Kir looked over his shoulder and pushed out a breath. "I think we'll be able to make it." Again, he was more talking to himself than her.

She almost asked where he was taking her and who he was bringing her to, but she didn't think he'd answer. She was nothing to him. If Viktor or one his guys didn't figure out where she was being forced to drive, she was going to have to get out of this on her own.

*　*　*

Ten minutes earlier

"Explain this as simply as possible," Viktor said to Lyosha, who'd just rushed them into his office because he said he had news. Both Lyosha and his brother could take forever to get to the point, especially when it had to do with Lyosha showing off his computer skills.

"All of the dead men were paid from a business account owned by a shell company." Lyosha set his laptop on Viktor's desk so he could see the spread of financial records.

Viktor only glanced at it. "You narrow down the owner yet?" Because that was all that mattered. Once Viktor had a name, the person who'd put Dominique in danger would pay.

"No, but I'm running a program that should help with that."

Viktor scrubbed a hand over his face. He'd been making calls the past hour, reaching out to contacts and calling in favors as he tried to narrow down who'd been stupid enough to attack him in his own hotel. So far his three top suspects weren't panning out. Two weren't even in the country and he knew without a doubt that if either had decided to make a move, they'd be here in person.

The third was dealing with the FBI on suspicion of fraud and illegal smuggling. According to the digging Viktor had done, the man was under almost twenty-four-hour surveillance so it seemed unlikely he was the one behind it either.

"Tell me you have something, then." Lyosha had called him in here—away from Dominique. He knew he needed to be focusing on finding who'd targeted him, but he didn't like being away from her even for a moment. Not after last night. Now that he'd gotten a taste of her he wasn't letting her go and he wasn't above binding her to him with sex.

"Maybe. I got some interesting hits on the financials I ran. Nothing on the phone records but I really didn't expect any. Even these financial records can be explained away, but you still need to see what I've found."

Viktor just grunted. If someone was going to betray him, they wouldn't be stupid enough to use their own phone.

Lyosha started to pull up another screen when his computer dinged. "Hold on," he murmured, his fingers moving quickly across the keyboard. His expression grew tighter, putting Viktor on alert.

They'd worked together a long, damn time. Something was wrong. He knew better than to ask though, until Lyosha was done working.

"Fuck," the other man growled. "Kir's the owner of one of the accounts from the unknown shell corporations."

Viktor froze. "Kir?" Their regular driver? A man he trusted.

Lyosha's expression was grim. "It's not on any of my current financials for him. He was careful to hide it but he's definitely receiving deposits from the same account the dead hit men did."

"Who's the owner?" he demanded, pulling out his cell phone to alert the rest of his security team. Kir was on the premises and he was going to be dealt with now.

"Still don't know—"

His phone buzzed in his hand. It was Dima, in charge of the perimeter security. He answered immediately. "What?"

"She's gone! I don't know if she was willing or not but I don't think she was. Kir and the woman came barreling out of the garage."

The bottom of his stomach fell out.

Viktor grabbed Lyosha's arm and motioned that he should follow. Lyosha was already on the phone, likely with another one of his guys. He grabbed his laptop and fell in behind Viktor.

Dima continued as Viktor raced through his house, his heart pounding out of control. Dominique was gone; she'd been taken. Because no way had she left willingly.

He needed to know where that bastard Kir had taken her—and why.

"Brady went to stop the SUV and she gunned it, tearing out of here. Brady thinks Kir meant to shoot him but can't be sure. He said she looked terrified. I managed to shoot out one of the tires."

"Where are you now?" he demanded as he burst through the door to the garage. Two of his security guys were standing in the driveway on their phones. He ignored them and got into the car. Lyosha slid into the passenger seat.

He was vaguely aware of Lyosha barking out orders to someone but he ignored him and focused on Dima as he tore out of the garage in his Tesla.

"I took off after them in one of the SUVs. I've got two guys with me. There's only one way he could have gone to escape... Shit."

Bolts of adrenaline pumped through his system. He clenched his fingers around the wheel, surprised he hadn't ripped the thing off the dash. "What?"

"Just found the SUV. It's abandoned."

"Where are you?"

"Gas station right before the highway." Dima's voice was tight.

Fuck, fuck, fuck. He lived in a private, cut off neighborhood but once you crossed the bridge to the mainland, there were too many damn directions Kir could have taken Dominique. And if he got on the highway... That fear compounded, making him imagine every horrific scenario possible for why Dominique had been taken, what could happen to her.

"We're going to find her." Lyosha's voice made his head jerk around and Viktor realized he was blindly driving in the direction of the gas station but not really seeing anything.

He'd never known what true fear could be until now. Even the times he'd been facing certain death he'd never been afraid like this. Because this was different. This was fear for the woman he loved. He wasn't afraid of his own death but the thought of her dying—no. It wasn't happening.

He'd get her back no matter what it took.

CHAPTER SEVENTEEN

Dominique opened her eyes, blinking against the brightness of the sun... No, not the sun. A spotlight. What the hell?

As the memory of everything came back, her stomach revolted. She'd been kidnapped and forced at gunpoint to drive to some building downtown. That was all she remembered before Kir clocked her in the side of the head. Then...blackness.

She tried to twist around but the movement sent pain splintering through her head. She bit back a groan, unsure if she was alone or not. If she wasn't she didn't want to draw attention to herself.

A new fear blasted through her as she looked down at herself. She was in a chair, her hands cuffed to the armrests and... She tried to lift her legs but her ankles were secured too. At least her clothes were still on.

Kir hadn't said much about why he was bringing her to someone but it was obviously not for a good reason.

Think, she ordered herself. The spotlight in her face was so damn bright that beads of sweat were trickling down her forehead. Blinking, she tried to see past the spotlight and could just make out some random shapes. No, not random... A couple chairs and...huge open windows. Just like in her office. It was hard to tell but she thought she could see a high-rise through the window. She couldn't be sure though.

She yanked against the cuffs and her chair scooted across the floor a couple inches. The scraping sound echoed slightly.

"Well, well, you're finally awake." Snapping footsteps across the concrete floor made her go still. "Smile for the camera, sweetheart."

* * *

Viktor slammed his fist against Kir's face again, the darkest part of him savoring the man's cry of agony as his nose broke—again. He reared back to hit him but Abram wrapped his arm around Viktor's neck and yanked him back, tackling him to the ground.

His brother had his arms and legs wrapped around him tight. "You kill him, you kill your chance to find her," Abram growled, struggling to hold Viktor in place. "Don't be stupid. Don't fail her."

The words rolled through him, bringing him back through the haze of his rage. Though it took effort, he stopped fighting his brother, expelling a ragged breath as he looked at Kir's prone body. He wasn't restrained, but he didn't attempt to get up. Not with Lyosha ten feet away on his laptop working furiously and two of Viktor's guys standing guard—men who'd been friends with Kir.

The fucking traitor. He'd betrayed them all.

"You really thought you could betray us and get away with it?" His voice was steady.

Abram loosened his grip and they both shoved to their feet.

"It wasn't supposed to be like this," Kir rasped out, his voice uneven. He'd ditched his cell phone but he hadn't ditched his laptop. Which was how they'd been able to track him.

One of his eyes was swollen shut, his nose broken in multiple places, and blood covered the front of his shirt as he stared up from the floor of the kitchen—in a condo that Lyosha had easily tracked him to. One of Kir's ankles was broken too, his foot twisted at an odd angle.

It wasn't enough. Viktor wanted to break every bone in his body with his bare hands when he thought of Dominique somewhere terrified for her life, being hurt... He locked the thought down before he broke Kir's neck. His brother was right. He needed to stay calm and find out where Dominique was.

He crouched down next to Kir's head. The man stared at him through his one good eye. "What was it supposed to be like?"

"I was just...giving him info about you. That's...it." He wheezed out the last couple words, his face scrunching in pain.

"Who?" Viktor just needed a name. The name of the man who'd orchestrated the kidnapping of the woman he loved. The man who'd turned one of his employees against him.

"You'll kill...me if...I tell you."

"I'm going to kill you anyway." He leaned closer to Kir, rage infusing him as he looked at the man who'd held Dominique at gunpoint, dragged her away from where she'd felt safe. Where she should have *been* safe. Viktor had no idea what Kir had done to her either. That not knowing was making him insane. "If you tell me I'll make your death quick. If you don't…you know what I used to do to people who crossed me."

The truth was, he'd never been into torture. Unlike his father. But he'd stoked the rumors of his nature years ago so people would be afraid to cross him. Clearly his reputation hadn't been enough to keep Kir from turning on him. Viktor would have to remedy that soon.

When Kir didn't respond, he continued. "See my man Lyosha over there? You know how good he is at finding people. He found you in less than an hour. He's already drained all your bank accounts—even the one you thought you'd hidden from us. Now all his focus is on finding who hired you. He *will* find who it is, that I have no doubt. The only question is, will he find him first or will you tell me? Because once he finds what I need, my offer of mercy is gone. I'll keep you alive for weeks. At least." He leaned even closer so that his mouth almost brushed Kir's ear. "I will cut you apart piece by piece. And then I will make you eat your own dick."

"Found something," Lyosha said

Eyes widening, Kir blurted, "Shane Hollis! He's the one who's been paying me! I took her…to one of his buildings downtown. The top four…floors are…" His breathing was labored and his words starting to slur. "Abandoned. He's keeping her there…for now." He rattled off an address before breaking into a fit of coughing.

Viktor shoved to his feet, looking to Lyosha for confirmation. His head of security shrugged and Viktor realized Lyosha hadn't found anything. He'd just been trying to goad Kir into talking.

It was hard to believe Hollis was behind this. The trust-fund jackass was so weak, ineffective at business—and had a drug problem.

"Keep him alive for now," Viktor said to Dima. He wasn't sure what he was going to do with Kir yet.

Dima nodded, giving Kir a look of pure disgust.

Viktor turned away, all thoughts of Kir's betrayal taking a backseat to finding Dominique. Saving her was all that mattered.

His phone buzzed in his pocket. He yanked it out, answered even though he didn't recognize the number. This could be about Dominique. "Hello?"

"Click on video capability," a distorted male voice said.

The fear inside him raked against his insides like savage, unforgiving talons. He motioned to his brother to keep Kir quiet as he quickly moved out of the kitchen. He stopped in the bare living room and swiped his thumb across the screen.

Dominique appeared, her face scrunched up. She was squinting. Her face was illuminated by a bright light. His throat seized in terror when he saw that she was cuffed to a chair, her arms and legs restrained.

Suddenly the light dimmed and a man wearing a hockey mask crouched next to her, his face right by hers as he fisted the long length of her hair and yanked her head back. The blade of a knife gleamed as he held it up in full view of the camera.

Crying out, she blinked, her eyes filling up with tears as she stared into the camera. He wanted to tell her everything would be okay, but he knew he'd break if he started down that road.

He had to keep his shit together for her, to get her out of this whole. "What do you want?" His voice was somehow calm.

"You took something that belonged to me. Now I have something that belongs to you." The voice was muffled but not mechanical. It was difficult to tell if it was Hollis or not. Leaning closer to the camera, the man loosened his grip on her hair but didn't let go completely as he moved forward.

"Tell me what you want and it's yours." He couldn't even negotiate. Not with Dominique's life in the balance. He'd give this monster whatever he wanted.

"You're going to meet with me at a place of my choosing and sign over property to me. If you involve the cops she's dead."

He snorted in derision. "There will be no police."

The masked man nodded once, setting the knife down. "You will also bring your brother. If you have any backup, however, she's dead. If I even *think* you have backup, she's fucking dead. And I'll amuse myself with her before I kill her." The man reached out and stroked Dominique's cheek. "She's got such a pretty mouth."

A red haze blurred Viktor's vision at the sight of this bastard touching her. "Where do you want me to go?" he bit out.

The man rattled off an address but didn't drop his hand as he continued stroking her cheek. "Don't you agree she's got a pretty mouth? I can think of—"

He screamed as Dominique bit his hand, her teeth sinking into his flesh and holding tight. He backhanded her with his free hand. Her head snapped back and the man hit her again. Her head lolled forward and her body stilled.

Raw terror jumped inside Viktor. Cursing, the man shoved his face in front of the screen so that Viktor couldn't see her anymore.

Viktor growled low in his throat, his hand clenching around his phone. He was going to kill the man. *Slowly.*

"You have twenty minutes to be at that address. Go in through the parking garage. Bring your brother. Or the bitch dies."

The screen went black before he could respond.

"It's a trap," Abram said, moving into the living room with Lyosha.

Viktor nodded once, agreeing. It had to be a trap. Abram and Lyosha had clearly heard everything and Lyosha was still working away on a tablet.

"I got a location on where he called you from," he said. "The phone is a burner but it pinged from a property Shane Hollis owns—for now. It's being foreclosed on. It's different than the address he gave you. On the other side of downtown. It'd take him more than twenty minutes to get there."

He had no time to make a decision. "Can you find out what kind of security the place has? The one he called from?" He was already moving toward the front door. They needed to have left ten minutes ago.

"I can try, but it'll take more than twenty minutes to disable it, if that's what you're thinking."

That was exactly what he was thinking. Hollis, or whoever was under that mask, wanted him to go to a specific address when he wasn't even there. It had to be a trap. "What about the place he wants us to go to?"

He, Abram and Lyosha spilled out into the hallway, talking as they ran to the elevators. His body was moving on autopilot, his only goal to get to his car and find Dominique.

"It's...also being foreclosed on. Owned by Hollis too. This fucker is losing everything his family built," Lyosha muttered.

Viktor's gut told him to go to the place the phone pinged from. As the elevator dinged at the bottom floor, the doors whooshing open, he looked at his brother, who'd been quiet. "If it was Lucy, what would you do?"

"Go with my instinct—which says the place he wants us to meet him is a fucking trap. Probably rigged with explosives or someone waiting to take us out. I think your girl is at the place his phone pinged from."

"Me too." He pulled out his phone again as they hurried into the parking garage of the condo complex Kir had thought was his hideout. He needed to get into that building undetected in twenty minutes and there was only one man he could think of who could make it happen.

It was time to collect his favor from Harrison Caldwell.

CHAPTER EIGHTEEN

Weapon in hand, Viktor stood outside the stairwell door to one of the top floors of the Hollis-owned building. Lyosha and Abram were silently waiting on the stairs as he confirmed one last time with Harrison that they were good to go.

"We've completely taken over the security feeds. The top eight floors aren't being monitored but there's no way to know if he saw you infiltrating from the parking garage. From this point forward if he does have security capability, he'll only see what we show him." Harrison's voice was clipped over the phone line.

Viktor nodded at Abram and Lyosha and they moved silently up the stairs. Instead of using the elevators they'd chosen the stairs so they wouldn't be seen. The building hadn't been finished—Hollis had run out of money—so there was no security in the stairwells either. Not that it would have stopped Viktor from coming here.

Nothing could do that. "Thank you."

"I've called in a favor to the PD. They're going to move on the other building as if there's a bomb threat."

Which there very well could be. Viktor had no idea what Hollis had in store for him and Abram at the meeting place he'd insisted on. "Wait until I've got Dominique safe." Because if the cops moved in and Dominique was in there instead, or if Hollis got wind of the police involvement, he could kill her.

Harrison snorted. "Contact me in fifteen minutes or I'm sending the cops in."

Viktor didn't bother responding, just ended the call and checked to make sure his phone was on silent. This was it. He, Lyosha and Abram were sweeping every floor, starting with the empty four on top.

Heart pounding, he eased open the door and peered into a hallway. Sunlight streamed in through the open doorways. A couple soda cans sat in a cluster near the closest entry—with no door. The floors weren't done; the steel and concrete frame was visible down the majority of the hallway. Insulation was also visible through the nearest open doorway, as if the construction crew had started installing it, then stopped mid-job.

He took a step into the hallway but froze at the slight echo of his footstep. Inwardly wincing, he slipped his shoes off and tucked them out of sight in the nearest room. Weapon up, he moved silently room to room, sweeping each one with a glance. There was no furniture, nothing to hide anyone.

When he heard a muffled sound three doors down from the opposite stairwell, he froze, listening. He heard it again.

It was too much to expect that it was Dominique, but the hope burst inside him, a burning wish to find her alive, unharmed.

He glanced once over his shoulder before continuing his path. His heart was an erratic tattoo against his chest as he moved like a predator hunting prey. If Hollis was in there, the man was dead. Viktor wouldn't allow him to surrender.

At the next doorway he heard the scraping, shuffling again. Moving in low, he swept the room with his weapon, immediately dropping it when he saw Dominique restrained to a chair, a gag in her mouth. Alone.

The spotlight was off her, at least.

Her eyes widened when she saw him. A bruise was forming on her cheek and a tiny trail of dried blood streaked down her chin, but she was alive. For the first time in the last hour he felt as if he could breathe again. Pistol still in his hand he hurried across the open room.

Crouching next to her, he turned so that he had the doorway in his periphery. He wanted to comfort her, but if Hollis was nearby Viktor didn't want the man to hear him. Holding a finger to his mouth, he then tugged her gag free. He didn't have a way to get the cuffs off, not without a key or a way to cut them free.

"He's crazy," she whispered. "He's got guys waiting at that other building. If Abram's gone there—"

"He hasn't. I'm going to get you out of here. I can't get these off yet. Do you know where he is?" He kept his voice pitched low.

She shook her head as tears spilled over her cheeks.

He cupped her cheek with his free hand and swiped them away. He wanted to pull her to him but couldn't risk the distraction, couldn't risk losing focus on their surroundings for a moment. "You're okay now," he said quietly before pulling his phone out. He needed to call

Harrison and get his brother and Lyosha up here. They needed to get Dominique free then hunt down Hollis.

Even killing that fucker took a backseat to getting her to safety. As the phone started to ring Shane Hollis stepped into the room, hockey mask shoved up on top of his head—and a pistol in his hand.

Viktor whipped his weapon up lightning fast, moving to stand directly in front of Dominique so that his body blocked hers entirely. "Drop your gun," Viktor ordered.

Hollis's eyes were wild, a little too big and red-rimmed. "You stupid fucker!"

"Drop your weapon. The police are on their way up. There's nowhere to go. Just put your gun down and you'll get out of this alive." The guy had hired men to come after Viktor and kidnapped Dominique so he was dead, regardless, but Viktor couldn't risk Dominique getting hurt or worse if the guy started firing.

"There are no cops!" His gun hand wavered slightly.

"Why did you do this? Why target me?" Viktor wanted to keep the guy talking. If the call to Harrison had connected, the other man should be hearing all this.

"You took everything from me!"

"I bought the businesses you put up for sale." *At a fair price*, he thought. Too fair, because he'd wanted to let the guy save some pride.

"Then you wouldn't work with me." His voice was whiny, matching the trust-fund jackass Viktor had pegged him for at their first meeting. "The fucking criminal wouldn't work with *me*. Me! I'm a fucking Hollis." His gun hand wavered. "My family built—"

Viktor pulled the trigger, hitting Hollis square in the chest. Hollis's eyes were wide as his body jerked back.

Boom. Boom.

Viktor fired again and again until Hollis tumbled backward, his weapon clattering to the concrete floor. He moved to it, kicked it away. Not bothering to check for a pulse, he patted the guy down until he found what he was looking for.

As he pulled the handcuff key out, he whipped his weapon up at a slight sound—then dropped it when he saw Abram and Lyosha rushing toward him.

Palming the key he hurried to Dominique, who was silently crying. After he'd freed her, she lunged at him before he could pull her into his arms.

"I thought he was going to kill you," she sobbed, her voice cracking. "He was so smug, so sure you'd walk right into his trap. He said...he said he was going to bring you here and make you watch as he—" Her voice broke then, her body racking with silent sobs as he lifted her into his arms. She wrapped her arms around his shoulders and buried her face against his neck as he carried her fireman-style out of the room. He couldn't move fast enough. He wanted her away from this death and pain.

"There's no one else here. Cops are on the way. So is Harrison," Abram said as Viktor stepped over Hollis's dead body.

"I'm taking her downstairs." Away from all this.

He didn't pause to talk to either Lyosha or his brother. The only thing that mattered was getting her to safety, getting her home—his home. Where no one would ever hurt her again.

He paused halfway down the hallway and turned to his brother. "Call Dima. Tell him to take care of it." Meaning Kir. No way was that fucker walking away after this. He wouldn't do jail time. He'd just disappear forever. But Viktor would make sure that word spread in the right circles that he'd died because of his betrayal. A gruesome, horrific death. He had no problem spreading false rumors about himself, not when those rumors would keep Dominique safe. So anyone who thought they might target him or his loved ones in the future would think twice.

"Already done. We'll make it look like—"

Viktor shook his head sharply to cut Abram off. He didn't want Dominique to hear any of this. She needed to be completely truthful in everything she said to the police. She was a victim and an employee of Red Stone Security so he had no doubt the police would treat her right. But he didn't want there to be any doubt about what had happened today.

She'd been kidnapped by Kir, then brought to Shane Hollis. For all the cops would think, Kir had disappeared, going on the run for his life. Viktor didn't want her to know what would happen to Kir—at least not until after she'd talked to the police.

CHAPTER NINETEEN

Abram shifted slightly against the bed, watching Lucy as she slept. Today had been a new level of insanity for him and his brother. And that was saying a lot.

After dealing with the cops and hours of endless questions and paperwork, Viktor and Dominique were holed up at Viktor's place and Abram had brought Lucy to his. He needed to know she was safe, protected.

And he wasn't going to let her go anytime soon—or ever. She might not realize it yet, but that necklace was only the first piece of jewelry he'd be buying her. Soon he planned to have a ring on her finger. All the muscles in his body were pulled taut, his cock rock hard, as he watched her. He should just get up, let her sleep, but he liked being near her.

He hadn't told his brother yet, but he was going to insist that they all take Monday off. Everyone could use a break, as far as he was concerned, and he planned on keeping Lucy on lockdown, naked and happy the entire day

"I can hear you thinking," Lucy murmured, not opening her eyes even as a seductive smile curved her lips. "Everything okay?"

"Yeah," he rasped out. He slid his palm under the sheet and over her bare stomach. He hadn't wanted to wake her before but touching her grounded him, reminded him that she was real and all his.

Cracking open her eyes, she turned, sliding her arm around his waist and pressing her bare chest to his. "You sure about that?"

He loved being skin to skin with her. Before Lucy he'd never had a woman at his place. Now...he wanted to wake up to her face every morning. It was a strange thing, this need to have her in his life, to see her every day. He'd felt this way since he'd met her but he still wasn't used to it. "Just thinking that it could have been you kidnapped this morning. Viktor kept his shit together better than I would have." It was a testament to his brother's control. Abram couldn't even imagine Lucy being stolen from him. It made his entire body break out in a sweat.

"Nah, you'd have taken care of business like you always do," Lucy murmured into his chest, her voice thick with sleep. "I'm just glad Dominique is okay. She's a good fit for your brother."

"Yeah, she is." And he felt like a bit of a dick for the way he'd talked about her to Viktor when it was clear the woman deeply cared for him. Not that he'd change his reaction. He'd just been looking out for his brother—and he'd do it again.

"So what's going to happen with Kir? You think the police will ever find him?" She leaned back a fraction, her hair rustling against the pillow as she met his gaze. She was slightly more awake now and he was glad—because he wasn't letting her go back to sleep until he'd gotten a taste of her.

"I think..." He paused, choosing his words carefully. "You don't need to worry about him ever again. He won't be a problem for us. I swear it. And...it's highly unlikely the police will find him." Abram felt no guilt that Kir was dead either. The man had betrayed him and his brother in the worst way possible.

Her eyes widened slightly then she shook her head, her expression wry. "I should probably be horrified by that, but I'm so freaking glad we don't have to worry about him." She yawned, stretching so that her back arched and her breasts rubbed against his chest again.

He'd been trying to show some restraint. He hadn't woken her up or pounced the moment he knew she was awake—but his self-control was pretty thin where she was concerned. He wanted to test her slickness then slide right into her. Fuck foreplay right now. He craved being inside Lucy.

Moving his hand lower, he cupped her pussy.

She sucked in a breath, her eyes going heavy-lidded with hunger. "You're a machine."

"I can stop if you want."

"Okay, stop," she whispered, watching him carefully, a grin pulling at her mouth.

He inwardly smiled. She wanted to play. He slid a finger inside her to find her slick. "You sure about that?" Breathing erratically, she shook her head so he added another finger. "I love you." The words were out before he could analyze them or try to talk himself out of saying them. He wasn't used to being vulnerable in front of anyone.

Her dark eyes widened and for a brief moment he worried he'd fucked up by moving too fast, but the smile she gave him was blinding. "I love you too, you sexy, frustrating Russian."

Relief like he'd never known surged through him, hearing the admission from her. Yeah, she was definitely his.

He nipped her bottom lip between his teeth, keeping his fingers buried inside her but not moving. For now, he just wanted to take his time with the woman he'd fallen in love with. Today had only cemented his feelings for Lucy. When he imagined what it would have been like to be in his brother's shoes, it clawed him up inside. He would never let anything happen to Lucy, never let anyone take her from him. She was his, and he was hers.

"You're taking Monday off. We're going to spend it in bed."

"Hmm, bossy, bossy," she murmured. "I'll take Monday off only if you promise to make it worth my time." The seductive grin she gave him made his cock jerk.

"I promise you'll want to call in sick Tuesday too," he murmured before capturing her mouth fully with his.

* * *

Dominique opened her eyes and groaned as she rolled over in Viktor's huge bed. After the insanity of today even her brain felt tired. The endless questions from the police, going through everything a dozen times, and then the worry that Viktor would somehow be in trouble for killing Shane Hollis was beyond overwhelming.

She'd thought she'd sleep until morning but it was only ten p.m. She'd only gotten about two hours of sleep. Frowning, she sat up in bed, the sharpest sense of disappointment hitting her that she was alone.

Sliding out of bed, she winced at the ache in her face. At least she didn't have any broken bones, just some bruising from the cuffs and on her cheek. And she and Viktor were alive, the only thing that mattered.

At first she was terrified when she'd learned that Kir, the man who'd kidnapped her, hadn't been located by the police, but Viktor had stressed that he wouldn't be a problem to her ever again. It hadn't been hard to read between the lines and the truth was, she didn't want to know what Viktor had done to him. She was just glad the guy was out of their lives.

She peeked into his office and found it empty so decided to go exploring. He wouldn't have left the house. Or she really hoped he hadn't.

A chill snaked through her as she stepped into the hallway, the wood floor cold against her feet. She knew the chill had nothing to do with the house though—she just couldn't seem to get warm. Viktor had already had her clothes brought to his place so at least she was in her own pajamas.

The only thing she really cared about was finding Viktor. He'd saved her and she was completely and utterly in love with him. She needed to tell him. It didn't matter if it was too soon or if he didn't return her feelings.

After a few minutes she found him in the kitchen, slightly bent over as he pulled something from one of the shelves in the refrigerator.

"That's a sight for sore eyes," she murmured, taking in the tight lines of his back and all those beautiful tattoos. The man should never, ever wear a shirt.

He jerked at her voice, a plastic container in his hands as he turned. "You're awake." He set it down on the island, hurrying to her side and practically carrying her to the nearest seat at the island.

"I'm okay," she murmured.

"I thought you'd be out for a while." Guilt flickered in his gaze. "I didn't want you to wake up alone."

"It's okay, seriously. I'm...actually kinda hungry."

"I was about to heat up chicken parm. You want some?"

"That sounds amazing." She'd only been able to stomach a little soup when they'd finally gotten back to Viktor's place. As if on cue, her stomach growled.

He half-smiled and brushed his mouth over hers. She felt it all the way to her toes, but he moved back too quickly for her to fully enjoy it.

"How does a glass of red wine sound? It might help you sleep since you won't take your medicine." His voice was slightly annoyed as he started scooping the food onto two plates.

The doctor who'd looked her over at the hospital had given her a prescription for pain meds, but she hadn't taken anything except ibuprofen. "That sounds good." It was weird seeing him acting so domestically, moving around the kitchen with such ease. "Did you cook this?"

He snorted and shot her an amused glance over his shoulder. "No. I have someone who comes in once or twice a week with casseroles and pre-makes things for me for the week."

She laughed lightly. "Can I help with anything?"

He simply frowned and turned to the microwave as it dinged. "You are not to do anything for at least a week."

"Pretty sure that's not what the doctor said."

"It's what I say." He pulled out the plate and tested it before bringing it over to her. "And you will follow orders." There was no command in his voice, more concern than anything else.

"If you hadn't just saved my life I might take issue with your bossiness," she murmured, taking the glass of wine he offered her.

"And you'll be staying here." There was no room for argument in his tone. He leaned against the island next to her seat, determination in his blue eyes as he looked down at her.

"For the next week?"

"Yes." There was something in his tone she couldn't quite read.

"I'd like that...if you're sure." Things between them had happened so quickly, and while she knew her feelings for him were true, she also didn't want him to get sick of her. He was such a hard man to read. Even though he'd made himself vulnerable with her a couple times, she still wasn't sure if his feelings for her were as strong.

His eyebrows pulled together. Instead of responding he turned and put his own plate in the microwave. "I've got security stationed around the house but no one inside. And Abram and Lucy have gone back to his place."

"I thought those two were together," she murmured, blowing on her food. "Any new developments I should know about?"

He shook his head and leaned against the counter, watching her with that brooding stare she found she liked way too much. "Nothing new."

"What's wrong, then?" Because she was coming to learn his moods, and right now something was bothering him. A lot. "We're not in danger, we're alone, and we've got awesome food."

He rounded the island and pushed right up into her personal space. She dropped her fork as he cupped her face in his hands, his hold so incredibly gentle it made her want to cry. "I keep seeing you tied up, him hitting you and..." He swallowed hard, the raw vulnerability on his face clawing at her.

Through everything that had happened, he'd been a rock. She'd been a complete sobbing mess once he'd gotten her out of that building. It was like the floodgates had opened and she just couldn't stop crying. She'd been so damn grateful to lean on him. He'd been next to her through all the police questions, stoic and unshakeable.

She moved off the chair, pulling him into a tight embrace, resting her head against his chest. "I'm not going anywhere. I'm here, safe, and nothing is going to happen to us again. I know I said it already but thank you for coming for me. Thank you for saving me. Thank you for being you. I...love you." She pulled back as she said the words, so she could see his face as she admitted the truth. "I'm not saying it because of what happened. I'm saying it because it's the truth. I love you, Viktor."

He stared down at her, as if he couldn't believe what she'd said. "I…" He cleared his throat. "You're moving in with me."

She blinked at his brusque tone as well as his words. "What?"

"I don't want you here for just the week. I want you here always." His big body was trembling under her hold and she realized this was how he was telling her that he loved her.

Or she really hoped that's what he meant. Because what she felt for him was consuming. She would need to hear the words eventually but for now, happiness bloomed in her chest. "We'll talk about it at the end of the week."

He just gave her a sensual look before brushing his mouth over hers in a teasing, stroking kiss that once again was over way too quickly. "Eat your food."

She did as he said, and once they were done he carried her to his bed where he tucked both of them in and wrapped his arm snug around her middle. She could feel the hard length of him pressed against her back but he made no move to do anything about it.

She was too exhausted anyway and she was grateful that he was simply holding her. She needed his strength.

"I love you too," he whispered against her hair a few moments later, his big body going rigid as he spoke. "And I'm not letting you go."

Hearing the words soothed all the ragged edges inside her. She linked her fingers through his, squeezed tight. "I'm not letting you go either," she murmured as she felt herself start to drift, knowing that she was safe in Viktor's arms.

Four months later

Dominique sat on the edge of her and Viktor's bed, watching him standing like a statue in their walk-in closet, staring at his clothes. He was only wearing pants, and she didn't mind the view. Still, the man normally just picked something in minutes. His clothes were obsessively organized anyway, unlike her side of the closet.

"I've never seen you like this," she murmured more to herself than him.

He'd pretty much steamrolled her into moving in with him four months ago—and the truth was she hadn't wanted to spend any nights away from him so it hadn't exactly been a hardship. Incredible sex every night and some mornings with the sweetest, sexiest man she was crazy in love with? *Yes, please.*

He turned to her and blinked, as if coming back to himself. "This is a big deal."

"You've met Quinn and Athena before." Her cousin Quinn had been unsure about Viktor at first, but considering he'd literally saved her life, Quinn had been mostly welcoming.

"Thanksgiving is different. And it's at Athena's family's house."

"Yeah, they're kind of insane, by the way." Athena came from a huge Greek family. One of Athena's cousins, Belle, Grant Caldwell's wife, was super pregnant and about to pop. "According to Athena everyone has a bet on when Belle will give birth. They seriously have a pool going."

Viktor scrubbed a hand over his face before he pulled a cashmere sweater from the closet. "I've never done a family holiday before. Even with Abram, we never do anything big." His brother was spending Thanksgiving with Lucy's family and she knew he was worried too.

Dominique slid off the bed at the surprising note of worry in Viktor's voice. Pretty much nothing rattled the man, but she shouldn't be surprised about this. He'd never even had a big birthday party, something she'd found out when she threw him a surprise party a month ago. He'd been stunned, and though he'd kept his serious, typically hard Russian expression in place most of the party, she'd known how pleased he'd been. Even Abram had been impressed with the party—and had finally warmed up to her. He'd even asked Dominique to help him pick out an engagement ring for Lucy, which pretty much told her that he completely trusted her now.

She pulled Viktor into a tight hug, burying her face against his chest before he tugged the sweater on. She could never seem to get enough of him. "Holiday stuff like this is usually fun. There's lots of food, maybe a little drinking and usually watching some stupid sports game on TV afterward."

He rested his chin on top of her head, sighed. "I'm not really worried about Thanksgiving."

Frowning, she pulled back. "What is it, then?" Fear slid through her veins when he didn't answer, just watched her with way too many emotions for her to decipher. He looked almost afraid. Oh God, was there another threat against them—

Abruptly he dropped to one knee and a jewelry box appeared in his hand as if out of thin air.

Her heart skipped a beat as she stared at him—and the box. She'd thought they were probably heading in this direction, but she hadn't expected this so soon. Though she had been hoping for it.

"I can't wait any longer," he rasped out. "I love you, Dominique. I never even thought I was capable of loving someone so much, but...you make me a better person, as stupid as it sounds."

"It doesn't sound stupid," she whispered, staring at his handsome face as he knelt there, the fear and hope on his face making her heart squeeze. She couldn't believe he was afraid though. He should know what her answer would be.

His eyes held hers. "Marry me?"

"Yes." She held out her left hand, only trembling a little as he slid a beautiful solitaire diamond on her finger. Then she fell to her knees, wrapping her arms around his neck as she slanted her mouth over his.

In pure Viktor style, he took over immediately, pinning her to the floor of their closet with a fierceness she craved from him.

When he slid his hands up her thighs, shoving her pretty red dress up to her waist, she knew that they were definitely going to be late. And she was more than okay with that.

Thank you for reading Love Thy Enemy. I really hope you enjoyed it and that you'll consider leaving a review at one of your favorite online retailers.

If you don't want to miss any future releases, please feel free to join my newsletter. I only send out a newsletter for new releases or sales news. Find the signup link on my website: http://www.katiereus.com

ACKNOWLEDGMENTS

Thank you to the normal crowd! Kari, Carolyn, Julia, Sarah, and Jaycee, thank you all for helping get this book ready for publication. For my readers, thank you for loving the Red Stone Security series as much as I do. It's because of you this series is going strong. For my family, as always, thanks for putting up with my crazy hours. Last but not least (always!) I'm grateful to God.

COMPLETE BOOKLIST

Non-series Romantic Suspense
Running From the Past
Dangerous Secrets
Killer Secrets
Deadly Obsession
Danger in Paradise
His Secret Past
Retribution
Merry Christmas, Baby

Paranormal Romance
Destined Mate
Protector's Mate
A Jaguar's Kiss
Tempting the Jaguar
Enemy Mine
Heart of the Jaguar

Moon Shifter Series
Alpha Instinct
Lover's Instinct (novella)
Primal Possession
Mating Instinct
His Untamed Desire (novella)
Avenger's Heat
Hunter Reborn
Protective Instinct (novella)

Darkness Series
Darkness Awakened
Taste of Darkness
Beyond the Darkness
Hunted by Darkness
Into the Darkness

ABOUT THE AUTHOR

Katie Reus is the *New York Times* and *USA Today* bestselling author of the Red Stone Security series, the Darkness series and the Deadly Ops series. She fell in love with romance at a young age thanks to books she pilfered from her mom's stash. Years later she loves reading romance almost as much as she loves writing it.

However, she didn't always know she wanted to be a writer. After changing majors many times, she finally graduated summa cum laude with a degree in psychology. Not long after that she discovered a new love. Writing. She now spends her days writing dark paranormal romance and sexy romantic suspense.

For more information on Katie please visit her website: www.katiereus.com. Also find her on twitter @katiereus or visit her on facebook at: www.facebook.com/katiereusauthor.

Made in the USA
Charleston, SC
22 October 2016